序　言

　　最近幾年，「文意選填」已成爲「大學入學學科能力測驗」及「大學入學指定科目考試」必考的題型。在各校的週考、月期考和模擬考試中，也會考類似的題型。所以我們的目標就是攻克「文意選填」，從現在開始，要練習、練習、再練習，在「學測」和「指考」中，這個大題的分數，一定要全部拿到手。

　　一般而言，「文意選填」的難度介於字彙題和克漏字之間，要拿高分，就是要不斷地練習。文意選填的空格通常是十個，選項也只有十個，所以就是一個空格一個答案。作答時，如果空格要填介系詞或副詞，可以用刪去法，把詞性不對的選項刪掉，再從剩下的選項中，選出最有可能的答案。

　　此外，要養成習慣，已經填過的選項就在試題卷上做個記號，這樣可以節省作答時間，也可以避免重複選同一個選項，白白丟掉分數。如果有某個空格，實在選不出答案，不用緊張，先跳過去，到最後看剩下哪個選項，再把它填進去，如果發現不適合填入，那就表示前面也有選錯，須再檢查一次。

練習就是得高分的秘訣

　　「文意選填」的作答要領，就是耐心與細心，因爲答案都在選項中，只要小心，要拿滿分並不難。在眞正考試時，時間非常有限，答題速度一定要快。所以，平時要多練習，訓練自己答得又快又正確。「**指考文意選填**」收集了各校月期考和模擬試題的精華，只要善用本書，先做題目，再研究詳解，「文意選填」將成爲你超越其他考生的秘密武器。

編者　謹識

TEST 1

說明： 第 1 至 10 題，每題一個空格。請依文意在文章後所提供的 (A) 到 (J) 選項中分別選出最適當者。

Most freshmen don't know ___1___ to plan their time when they first enter college. They are impressed ___2___ the large number of social activities listed in the college newspaper. And the result is they might fail if they want to ___3___ all of them. The older students try to warn them ___4___ the difficulties, but they ___5___ believe what other people say. Later they ___6___ what happens and they ___7___ they had taken the advice of the older students.

How freshmen ___8___ their time is very important. That all work and no play makes Jack a dull boy is a fact expressed ___9___ practically every language. Whoever wants to succeed should plan his time carefully and ___10___ to his plan.

(A) attend   (B) stick   (C) budget   (D) of
(E) wish   (F) how   (G) in   (H) regret
(I) by   (J) seldom

TEST 1 詳解

Most freshmen don't know ¹**(F) how** to plan their time when they first enter college. They are impressed ²**(I) by** the large number of social activities listed in the college newspaper. And the result is that they might fail if they want to ³**(A) attend** all of them. The older students try to warn them ⁴**(D) of** the difficulties, but they ⁵**(J) seldom** believe what other people say. Later they ⁶**(H) regret** what happens and they ⁷**(E) wish** they had taken the advice of the older students.

大部分的大一新生，都不知道他們上大學時，要如何去規劃他們的時間。他們對於刊登在校刊上眾多的社團活動印象深刻。結果是如果他們所有活動都想參加，可能就會當掉。學長們試著去警告他們這些難處，但是他們卻很少採信別人所說的話。之後，他們對於所發生的事，後悔不已，並且希望當時採納學長的建議就好了。

> freshman〔'frɛʃmən〕*n.* 大一新生　　plan〔plæn〕*v.* 規劃
> college〔'kɑlɪdʒ〕*n.* 大學
> ***be impressed by*** 對～印象深刻　　***the large number of*** 大量的
> ***social activity*** 社團活動　　list〔lɪst〕*v.* 刊登
> ***college newspaper*** 校刊　　result〔rɪ'zʌlt〕*n.* 結果
> difficulty〔'dɪfə,kʌltɪ〕*n.*（當可數名詞）難處；麻煩事
> advice〔əd'vaɪs〕*n.* 建議　　***take the advice*** 採納建議

1.(**F**)　大一新生不知要「如何」規劃他們的時間，選 (F) ***how***，表方法。

2.(**I**)　***be impressed by*** 對～印象深刻（= *be impressed with*）

3.(**A**)　根據句意，結果「參加」所有活動，他們可能會當掉，選 (A) ***attend***〔ə'tɛnd〕*v.* 參加。

4. (**D**) ***warn sb. of sth.*** 警告某人某事

5. (**J**) 大一新生「很少」相信別人說的話，選 (J) ***seldom***，強調頻率不高。

6. (**H**) 依句意，他們之後會對所發生的事感到「後悔」，選 (H) ***regret*** 〔 rɪˋgrɛt 〕 *v.* 後悔；遺憾。

7. (**E**) 依句意，他們「希望」那時候採納學長的建議就好了，選 (E) ***wish***，之後子句要採用假設語氣。

How freshmen ^{8}**(C) budget** their time is very important. That all work and no play makes Jack a dull boy is a fact expressed ^{9}**(G) in** practically every language. Whoever wants to succeed should plan his time carefully and ^{10}**(B) stick** to his plan.

大一學生要如何安排他們的時間，是非常重要的。幾乎每一種語言都有表達「只工作而不遊戲，會使人變得遲鈍，」這個事實。凡是想要成功的人，都應該謹慎規劃時間，並且堅持他的計劃。

All work and no play makes Jack a dull boy.
【諺】只工作而不遊戲，會使人變得遲鈍。
dull 〔 dʌl 〕 *adj.* 遲鈍的　　　express 〔 ɪkˋsprɛs 〕 *v.* 表達
practically 〔ˋpræktɪkḷɪ 〕 *adv.* 幾乎 (= *almost*)

8. (**C**) 要如何「安排」他們的時間，這一點很重要，選 (C) ***budget*** 〔ˋbʌdʒɪt 〕 *v.* 安排。

9. (**G**) 「*in* + 語言」，用來表示「用～語言」，選 (G)。

10. (**B**) ***stick to*** 堅持

TEST 2

說明： 第 1 至 10 題，每題一個空格。請依文意在文章後所提供的 (A) 到 (J) 選項中分別選出最適當者。

One of the changing aspects of American society is the growing trend of home education. A government survey ___1___ in 1990-1991 shows that between 250,000 and 300,000 children were taught at home. Another study made by a private foundation ___2___ that the current figure may be as high as one million. The number of parent-taught children is increasing ___3___ 15-20% annually, and it will continue to increase as more parents become dissatisfied ___4___ public school education and choose to teach their children at home.

Home education is legal in all American states, and each state sets its own laws ___5___ home education. In some states, parents need only to inform the city or town school board ___6___ their intention to teach their children at home.

On the other hand, there are people who are opposed __7__ home schooling. They claim that children who are taught at home have little or no __8__ with other children of the same age. They fear, __9__, that children will have no chance to learn the basic social skills which will be important when they become adults.

Generally speaking, __10__, children who are taught by their parents have frequently scored above national averages on achievement tests. Indeed, hundreds of colleges and universities around the country have accepted such students.

(A) concerning   (B) therefore   (C) with

(D) however   (E) at a rate of (F) contact

(G) indicates   (H) conducted   (I) to

(J) of

TEST 2 詳解

One of the changing aspects of American society is the growing trend of home education. A government survey [1](H) conducted in 1990-1991 shows that between 250,000 and 300,000 children were taught at home. Another study made by a private foundation [2](G) indicates that the current figure may be as high as one million.

> 美國社會許多方面一直在改變，其中之一就是在家自學的風潮，這個風潮愈來愈盛行。一項在一九九〇到一九九一年之間，由政府所做的調查顯示，大約有二十五萬到三十萬個學生是在家自學的。另外一項由某個私人基金會所做的研究顯示，目前在家自學的人數可能高達一百萬人。

> aspect ('æspɛkt) *n.* 方面　　growing ('groɪŋ) *adj.* 增加的
> trend (trɛnd) *n.* 風潮；趨勢
> **home education** 在家自學
> survey ('sɝve) *n.* 調查　　private ('praɪvɪt) *adj.* 私人的
> foundation (faʊn'deʃən) *n.* 基金會
> current ('kɝənt) *adj.* 現今的　　figure ('fɪgjɚ) *n.* 數目

1. (**H**) ***conduct a survey*** 進行調查
   conduct (kən'dʌkt) *v.* 進行，在此 conducted in 1990-1991 為形容詞片語，修飾先行詞 survey。

2. (**G**) 本句缺乏動詞，依句意，另外一個研究「顯示」目前人數可能高達一百萬人，故選 (G) ***indicates*** ('ɪndə,kets) *v.* 顯示。

The number of parent-taught children is increasing [3](E) at a rate of 15-20% annually, and it will continue to increase as more parents become dissatisfied [4](C) with public school education and choose to teach their children at home.

由父母親自授課的兒童人數，每年以百分之十至百分之二十的速度在成長，而這個數目還會持續增加，原因是因爲有愈來愈多父母，對公立學校的制度感到不滿，他們選擇在家裡自己教小孩。

annually〔'ænjʊəlɪ〕*adv.* 每年地
dissatisfied〔 dɪs'sætɪs,faɪd〕*adj.* 不滿的
public school 公立學校

3. (**E**) ***at a rate of*** 以～速度

4. (**C**) ***become dissatisfied with*** 對～變得不滿

Home education is legal in all American states, and each state sets its own laws [5](A) concerning home education. In some states, parents need only to inform the city or town school board [6](J) of their intention to teach their children at home.

在家自學在美國各州都是合法的，每一個州都會制定關於在家自學的法律。在某些州，父母甚至只需告知當市或當鎮的教育委員會，他們想在家裡自己教小孩就可以了。

legal〔'ligl〕*adj.* 合法的　　　***set laws*** 制定法律
inform〔 ɪn'fɔrm〕*v.* 通知　　***school board*** 教育委員會
intention〔 ɪn'tɛnʃən〕*n.* 意圖

5. (**A**) 依句意,各州可以制定「有關」在家自學的法律,故選
(A) *concerning* 〔kənˈsɝnɪŋ〕 *prep.* 有關。

6. (**J**) *inform sb. of sth.* 通知某人某事

On the other hand, there are people who are opposed [7](I) to
home schooling. They claim that children who are taught at home
have little or no [8](F) contact with other children of the same age.

可是另一方面,還是有人反對在家自學。他們認爲在家自學的小
孩,很少、或者根本就無法接觸其他同齡的小孩。

> *on the other hand* 另一方面　　oppose 〔əˈpoz〕 *v.* 反對
> *home schooling* 在家自學　　claim 〔klem〕 *v.* 宣稱

7. (**I**) *be opposed to* + *V-ing* / *N.* 反對

8. (**F**) 依句意,反對人士擔心,在家自學的小孩少有機會「接觸」同
齡小孩,故選 (F) *contact* 〔ˈkɑntækt〕 *n.* 接觸。

They fear, [9](B) therefore, that children will have no chance to
learn the basic social skills which will be important when they
become adults.

因此他們擔心,這些小孩沒有機會學習基本社交技巧,而這些社交技
巧對他們長大成人後,是相當重要的。

> *social skill* 社交技巧

9.(**B**) 由前句可知，反對人士擔心，在家自學的小孩少有機會接觸同
齡小孩，「因此」擔心他們學不到社交技巧，前後為因果關係，
故選 (B) *therefore*。

Generally speaking, [10](D) <u>however</u>, children who are taught
by their parents have frequently scored above national averages
on achievement tests. Indeed, hundreds of colleges and
universities around the country have accepted such students.

然而，就一般來說，在家自學的小孩在學科能力測驗中，分數通常
都在全國平均以上。事實上，全國有數百所學院和大學，都接受這種在
家自學的學生。

generally speaking 一般來說
frequently (ˈfrikwəntlɪ) *adv.* 經常
score (skor) *v.* 得（分）   ***above average*** 在平均以上
achievement test 學科能力測驗
around the country 全國

10.(**D**) 由前段可知，許多人認為在家自學有缺點，「然而」在家自
學的小孩成績都在平均以上，前後為轉折語氣，故選 (D)
however。

註：本題的選項中，只有兩個連接詞，即 (B) therefore 和 (D)
however，當你不知道該選哪個選項時，仔細觀察前後文是
最有效的方式。

TEST 3

說明：第 1 至 10 題，每題一個空格。請依文意在文章後所提供的 (A) 到
(J) 選項中分別選出最適當者。

Is eating between meals really so bad? Not
necessarily. In fact, many experts in nutrition say that
snacking is important for children, especially younger
and active children. Kids burn up calories ___1___
than adults; but at the same time, children usually eat
___2___ than adults at mealtimes because their stomachs
are smaller. So children actually need to have snacks
between meals.

But ___3___ snacking is good or bad really depends
on ___4___ you snack on. If you reach for cookies,
candy, and potato chips, you just fill up on empty
calories. And because these junk foods are high in sugar
and fat, they are more likely to ___5___ your appetite for
your next meal. You'll eat less, and ___6___ you may
not get the nutrients you need.

Does all this mean that you should never eat another candy bar, swear off hamburgers forever, or never let a potato chip touch your lips? Not at all. It just means that you should ___7___ a careful eye on what you eat — and ___8___ eating too much junk food. If you're getting the nutrients you need from healthy foods like fresh fruit, vegetables, and whole grain cereals, you'll have room in your diet for a candy bar or a few potato chips now and ___9___. The important thing is not to ___10___ it.

(A) what (B) keep (C) spoil

(D) thus (E) overdo (F) whether

(G) faster (H) avoid (I) then

(J) less

TEST 3 詳解

Is eating between meals really so bad? Not necessarily. In fact, many experts in nutrition say that snacking is important for children, especially younger and active children. Kids burn up calories [1](G) faster than adults; but at the same time, children usually eat [2](J) less than adults at mealtimes because their stomachs are smaller. So children actually need to have snacks between meals.

　　吃點心真的不好嗎？不一定。事實上，許多營養方面的專家都說，吃點心對兒童來說，是很重要的，特別是年紀較小、及活動力強的小孩。兒童燃燒卡路里的速度比成人快，但同時，兒童在用餐時間通常吃得比成人少，因為他們的胃比較小。因此，兒童實際上是需要吃點心的。

> ***eat between meals*** 吃點心　　***not necessarily*** 不一定
> nutrition〔nju'trɪʃən〕*n.* 營養
> snack〔snæk〕*v.* 吃點心　*n.* 點心
> ***burn up*** 燃燒；燒完　　calorie〔'kælərɪ〕*n.* 卡路里（熱量單位）
> mealtime〔'mil,taɪm〕*n.* 用餐時間

1. (**G**) 依句意，兒童燃燒卡路里速度「比較快」，選 (G) *faster*。

2. (**J**) 兒童的胃較小，所以吃得「較少」，選 (J) *less*。

But [3](F) whether snacking is good or bad really depends on [4](A) what you snack on. If you reach for cookies, candy, and potato chips, you just fill up on empty calories.

但是，吃點心是好是壞，其實是視你吃什麼而定。如果你伸手拿來
吃的是餅乾、糖果、洋芋片，你只是塞滿了無用的卡路里。

depend on 視~而定　　*reach for* 伸手去拿
potato chips 洋芋片　　*fill up* 塞滿；裝滿

3. (**F**) 由空格後面的 good or bad 可知，此處應用 *whether*，選 (F)。

4. (**A**) 依句意，吃點心的好壞視你吃「什麼」而定，選 (A) *what*。

And because these junk foods are high in sugar and fat, they are
more likely to [5](**C**) spoil your appetite for your next meal. You'll
eat less, and [6](**D**) thus you may not get the nutrients you need.
而且，因為這些垃圾食物的糖分和脂肪量都很高，它們更有可能破壞你下
一餐的食慾。你會吃得較少，而因此得不到你所需的養分。

junk food 垃圾食物　　*be likely to* + *V.* 可能
appetite ('æpə,taɪt) *n.* 食慾　　nutrient ('njutrɪənt) *n.* 養分

5. (**C**) *spoil* (spɔɪl) *v.* 破壞

6. (**D**) 你吃得較少，「因此」會得不到所需的養分，選 (D) *thus*。

Does all this mean that you should never eat another candy
bar, swear off hamburgers forever, or never let a potato chip touch
your lips? Not at all. It just means that you should [7](**B**) keep a
careful eye on what you eat — and [8](**H**) avoid eating too much
junk food.

這一切難道表示，你應該從此不能再吃棒棒糖，發誓永遠戒掉漢堡，或是再也不能讓洋芋片沾唇嗎？一點也不。這只是意味著，你應該要仔細注意你的飲食，避免吃太多垃圾食物。

> mean〔min〕*v.* 意味著
>
> ***candy bar*** 棒棒糖　　swear〔swɛr〕*v.* 發誓
>
> ***swear off*** 發誓戒掉（煙、酒等）
>
> lip〔lɪp〕*n.* 嘴唇　　***not at all*** 一點也不

7.(**B**) ***keep an eye on~*** 注意

8.(**H**) 依句意，要「避免」吃大多垃圾食物，選 (H) ***avoid***。

If you're getting the nutrients you need from healthy foods like fresh fruit, vegetables, and whole grain cereals, you'll have room in your diet for a candy bar or a few potato chips now and [9](I) then. The important thing is not to [10](E) overdo it.

如果你已經從健康的食物，像蔬菜水果、及五穀雜糧食品中，得到足夠的養分，那麼在你的飲食中，就還有空間，偶爾吃根棒棒糖或一點洋芋片。最重要的是，不要過量。

> grain〔gren〕*n.* 穀類　　cereal〔'sɪrɪəl〕*n.* 穀類食品
>
> ***whole grain cereals*** 五穀雜糧食品
>
> room〔rum〕*n.* 空間　　diet〔'daɪət〕*n.* 飲食

9.(**I**) ***now and then*** 偶爾

10.(**E**) ***overdo***〔,ovə'du〕*v.* 做太多；過分

TEST 4

說明： 第 1 至 10 題，每題一個空格。請依文意在文章後所提供的 (A) 到
(J) 選項中分別選出最適當者。

Suppose you ate a ___1___ cheese sandwich, a cup of
vegetable soup, and a fruit salad for lunch. Your meal
contained five essential ___2___ — carbohydrates, proteins,
fats, vitamins, and minerals.

Carbohydrates (___3___ and sugars) supply ___4___
energy needed for physical activity and other body ___5___.
Proteins repair and build body ___6___. Fats provide the
body's main source of energy during rest and ___7___
activities. In addition, fats are an important component
of cell membranes. Vitamins and minerals ___8___ body
functions.

In addition to those mentioned above, you need fiber.
Fiber consists of food particles that your body is unable to
___9___; it helps to push food through the ___10___ and to
eliminate wastes from the body.

(A) digest   (B) grilled   (C) intestines   (D) quick

(E) starches   (F) tissues   (G) functions   (H) nutrients

(I) light   (J) regulate

TEST 4 詳解

Suppose you ate a [1](B) grilled cheese sandwich, a cup of
vegetable soup, and a fruit salad for lunch. Your meal contained
five essential [2](H) nutrients —— carbohydrates, proteins, fats,
vitamins, and minerals.

假設你午餐吃了一個碳烤乳酪三明治，一杯蔬菜湯，一份水果沙拉。
你這一餐包含了五大基本營養素—— 醣類、蛋白質、脂肪、維他命以及礦
物質。

suppose〔sə'poz〕v. 假設
contain〔kən'ten〕v. 包含
essential〔ə'sɛnʃəl〕adj. 基本的
carbohydrate〔ˏkɑrbo'haɪdret〕n. 醣類；碳水化合物
protein〔'protiɪn〕n. 蛋白質　　fat〔fæt〕n. 脂肪
vitamin〔'vaɪtəmɪn〕n. 維他命
mineral〔'mɪnərəl〕n. 礦物質

1. (**B**) 午餐吃一個「碳烤的」乳酪三明治，選 (B) *grilled*〔grɪld〕adj.
   碳烤的。

2. (**H**) 醣類、蛋白質、脂肪、維他命以及礦物質是五大基本「營養
   素」，選 (H) *nutrients*〔'njutrɪənts〕n. pl. 營養素。

Carbohydrates ([3](E) starches and sugars) supply [4](D) quick
energy needed for physical activity and other body [5](G) functions.
Proteins repair and build body [6](F) tissues.

　　醣類（如澱粉和糖），提供最快速取得的能量，以供身體活動及其他身體機能之所需。蛋白質修護及建造身體組織。

　　sugar（ˋʃʊgɚ）*n.* 糖　　　supply（səˋplaɪ）*v.* 供應
　　energy（ˋɛnɚdʒɪ）*n.* 能量　　physical（ˋfɪzɪkḷ）*adj.* 身體的
　　repair（rɪˋpɛr）*v.* 修護

3. (**E**)　醣類包括「澱粉」和糖，選 (E) ***starch***（startʃ）*n.* 澱粉。

4. (**D**)　醣類最「最快消化」，故選 (D) ***quick***（kwɪk）*adj.* 最快的；最容易的。

5. (**G**)　醣類提供身體活動及其他身體「機能」所需要的熱量，選 (G) ***functions***（ˋfʌŋkʃənz）*n. pl.* 機能。

6. (**F**)　蛋白質修護及建造身體「組織」，選 (F) ***tissues***（ˋtɪʃuz）*n. pl.* 組織。

Fats provide the body's main source of energy during rest and ⁷(I) light activities. In addition, fats are an important component of cell membranes. Vitamins and minerals ⁸(J) regulate body functions.

脂肪提供身體休息和輕微活動時，主要的能量來源。此外，脂肪是細胞膜重要的成分。維他命和礦物質則調節身體機能。

　　source（sors,sɔrs）*n.* 來源　　　***in addition*** 此外
　　component（kəmˋponənt）*n.* 成分　　cell（sɛl）*n.* 細胞
　　membrane（ˋmɛmbren）*n.* 薄膜
　　regulate（ˋrɛgjəˏlet）*v.* 調節

7. (**I**) 脂肪提供休息時的能量，可見「輕微」活動（而非劇烈活動）也靠脂肪提供能量來源，選 (I) *light* 〔 laɪt 〕 *adj.* 輕量的。

8. (**J**) 維他命和礦物質則「調節」身體機能，選 (J) *regulate* 〔'rɛgjə,let 〕 *v.* 調節。

In addition to those mentioned above, you need fiber. Fiber consists of food particles that your body is unable to [9](A) digest; it helps to push food through the [10](C) intestines and to eliminate wastes from the body.

除了以上所提到的營養素，你還需要纖維。纖維是由體內不能消化的食物分子所組成的；它有助於推動食物，經過大、小腸，將身體中的廢物清除掉。

> *in addition to* 除了　　mention 〔'mɛnʃən 〕 *v.* 提到
> fiber 〔'faɪbɚ 〕 *n.* 纖維　　*consist of* 組成
> particle 〔'pɑrtɪkl̩ 〕 *n.* 分子　　*be unable to* 不能
> eliminate 〔 ɪ'lɪmə,net 〕 *v.* 清除　　waste 〔 west 〕 *n.* 廢物

9. (**A**) 纖維組成你身體不能「消化」的食物分子，所以才須清除，選 (A) *digest* 〔 daɪ'dʒɛst 〕 *v.* 消化。

10. (**C**) 纖維有助於推動食物，經過大、小「腸」，選 (C) *intestines* 〔 ɪn'tɛstɪnz 〕 *n. pl.* 腸。

TEST 5

說明： 第 1 至 10 題，每題一個空格。請依文意在文章後所提供的 (A) 到 (J) 選項中分別選出最適當者。

Over the last few decades, people's working lives have changed dramatically. In the past, unless you were ___1___ off for some reason, you expected to stay in the same job for quite a few years. Nowadays jobs are much less ___2___. As companies try to save as much money as they can, ___3___ are made redundant in their thousands. It is not ___4___, then, that many older people decide to start up their own small businesses ___5___ trying to find another job in someone else's. Being self-employed certainly has ___6___ advantages: you don't have to take orders from anyone else, and if you make a ___7___, you can keep it all for yourself. However, if you have had no previous ___8___ of running your own business, it's very easy to make mistakes. One common mistake is to offer a service for which there is little or no ___9___. A business that repairs faulty TV sets, for example, is ___10___ to do well in an area where most people would rather buy new TVs than have their old TVs repaired.

(A) unlikely   (B) profit   (C) demand   (D) experience
(E) secure   (F) laid   (G) surprising (H) its
(I) instead of (J) employees

TEST 5 詳解

Over the last few decades, people's working lives have changed dramatically. In the past, unless you were [1](F) laid off for some reason, you expected to stay in the same job for quite a few years. Nowadays jobs are much less [2](E) secure. As companies try to save as much money as they can, [3](J) employees are made redundant in their thousands. It is not [4](G) surprising, then, that many older people decide to start up their own small businesses [5](I) instead of trying to find another job in someone else's.

在過去幾十年來，人們的工作生涯已經大大地改變了。在過去，除非你是爲了某種原因被解雇，否則同一份工作預計可以待上好幾年。現在工作沒那麼穩定了。由於公司試著盡量省錢，員工若達到上千人時，就有冗員出現。因此，許多較老的員工決定自行創立小型企業，而不願到別人的公司找新工作，也就不足爲奇了。

> decade〔ˈdɛked〕*n.* 十年
> dramatically〔drəˈmætɪklɪ〕*adv.* 戲劇性地；大大地
> redundant〔rɪˈdʌndənt〕*adj.* 多餘的

1. (**F**) *lay off*「解雇」，在此爲被動，故選 (F) *laid*。

2. (**E**) *secure*〔sɪˈkjur〕*adj.* 安全的；穩固的

3. (**J**) *employee*〔ˌɛmplɔɪˈi〕*n.* 員工

4. (**G**) 依句意，這個現象並不「令人驚訝」，選 (G) *surprising*。

5. (**I**) 老員工寧願自行創業，「而不」到別人的公司找新工作，選 (I) *instead of*。

Being self-employed certainly has ⁶**(H) its** advantages: you don't
have to take orders from anyone else, and if you make a ⁷**(B) profit**,
you can keep it all for yourself.　However, if you have had no
previous ⁸**(D) experience** of running your own business, it's very
easy to make mistakes.　One common mistake is to offer a service
for which there is little or no ⁹**(C) demand**.　A business that repairs
faulty TV sets, for example, is ¹⁰**(A) unlikely** to do well in an area
where most people would rather buy new TVs than have their old
TVs repaired.

自己當老板當然有它的優點在：你不必接受其他人的命令，而且如果賺錢
的話，你可以自己全部留下來。然而，你之前如果沒有自己經營事業的經
驗，就很容易犯錯。有一個常見的錯誤是，你所提供的服務，需求量很小
或沒有。例如在某地區，若大部分人寧願買新電視，也不願把舊電視送修，
那麼修理故障電視的生意，就不可能做得好。

　　self-employed (ˈsɛlfɪmˈplɔɪd) *adj.* 不受雇於他人的；自己經營的
　　advantage (ədˈvæntɪdʒ) *n.* 優點
　　take orders from sb. 接受某人的命令
　　previous (ˈpriviəs) *adj.* 以前的　　run (rʌn) *v.* 經營
　　faulty (ˈfɔltɪ) *adj.* 有缺點的；故障的
　　would rather ~ than… 寧願 ~ 而不願…

6. (**H**) 依句意，自己當老板當然有「它的」優點在，選 (H) ***its***。

7. (**B**) ***profit*** (ˈprɑfɪt) *n.* 利潤　　***make a profit*** 有利潤；賺錢

8. (**D**) 依句意，沒有「經驗」就容易犯錯，選 (D) ***experience***。

9. (**C**) ***demand*** (dɪˈmænd) *n.* 需求量

10. (**A**) ***be unlikely to*** + *V.* 不可能

TEST 6

說明： 第 1 至 10 題，每題一個空格。請依文意在文章後所提供的 (A) 到 (J) 選項中分別選出最適當者。

If you can't travel to visit a museum, maybe a museum will travel to visit you. That's the ___1___ behind Artrain, which is a museum in a train ___2___ of five silver-painted cars. It brings art to towns and cities throughout the United States.

Artrain was started in 1971 in the state of Michigan. Since ___3___ it has traveled to more than 500 towns and opened its doors to 2.5 million visitors. It has carried a total of 13 different shows. The latest, a collection of works from the Smithsonian Institution, is on a three-year national ___4___. People can see prints ___5___ famous artists in three of the train's cars. The fourth car holds a studio ___6___ artists show visitors how they work.

Artrain doesn't have an engine. Instead, it is
___7___ to regular trains and brought from one town
to the next. The train's stops are planned carefully,
___8___ special events and school visits in mind.
Arranging a traveling show like this is hard work,
but local volunteers work with the train staff to help
make each stop a ___9___. When Artrain arrives in
a town, kids and adults line up to see the treasures
inside. For many of the youngsters, especially, it is
their first visit to an art museum. And when they step
down from the last car, their most common ___10___
is "Let's go through again!"

(A) reaction   (B) connected   (C) where
(D) then   (E) by   (F) tour
(G) consisting   (H) idea   (I) with
(J) success

TEST 6 詳解

If you can't travel to visit a museum, maybe a museum will travel to visit you. That's the **[1](H) idea** behind Artrain, which is a museum in a train **[2](G) consisting** of five silver-painted cars. It brings art to towns and cities throughout the United States.

　　如果你無法前去博物館參觀，也許博物館會親自來拜訪你。這就是「藝術列車」背後的構想，藝術列車其實是一個位於火車內的博物館，由五個漆成銀色的車廂所組成。它把藝術帶到全美國的大小城鎮。

　　artrain ('ɑr,tren) *n.* 藝術列車 (是由 art「藝術」和 train「火車」
　　　所合成的字)
　　silver-painted ('sɪlvɚ'pentɪd) *adj.* 漆成銀色的
　　car (kɑr) *n.* 車廂

1. (**H**) 依句意，這就是藝術列車背後的「構想」，故選 (H) *idea*。

2. (**G**) 依句意，藝術列車是由五個銀色車廂所「組成」的火車，故選
　　　(G) *consisting*。此處 consisting…cars 爲形容詞片語，修飾先
　　　行詞 train。　*consist of* 由～組成

　　Artrain was started in 1971 in the state of Michigan. Since **[3](D) then** it has traveled to more than 500 towns and opened its doors to 2.5 million visitors. It has carried a total of 13 different shows. The latest, a collection of works from the Smithsonian Institution, is on a three-year national **[4](F) tour**.

藝術列車於一九七一年創始於密西根州。從那時起，它已行經五百多個城鎮，並開放給二百五十萬人參觀了。這部列車總共舉辦過十三個不同的展覽。目前最新的展覽，是爲期三年的全國巡迴展，當中的作品都是由史密森學會所收藏。

state〔stet〕*n.* 州
Michigan〔'mɪʃəgən〕*n.* 密西根州
carry〔'kærɪ〕*v.* 維持；主辦
different〔'dɪfərənt〕*adj.* 不同的
show〔ʃo〕*n.* 展覽 *v.* 展示 latest〔'letɪst〕*adj.* 最新的
collection〔kə'lɛkʃən〕*n.* 收藏
work〔wɜk〕*n.* 作品 institution〔ˌɪnstə'tjuʃən〕*n.* 協會
Smithsonian Institution 史密森學會（美國一著名文教機構）
national〔'næʃənl̩〕*adj.* 全國的

3. (**D**) *since then* 「自那時以來」。then 當代名詞用，表「那時」，這裡指一九七一年。

4. (**F**) 最近的展出目前正在全國「巡迴展覽」中，故選 (F) *tour*〔tʊr〕*n.* 巡迴展覽。

People can see prints ⁵(E) by famous artists in three of the train's cars. The fourth car holds a studio ⁶(C) where artists show visitors how they work.

參觀者可以在其中三節車廂，欣賞到知名藝術家的作品。第四個車廂裡有一個工作室，參觀者可以在那裡看到藝術家創作的過程。

print〔prɪnt〕*n.* 作品 artist〔'ɑrtɪst〕*n.* 藝術家
studio〔'stjudɪˌo〕*n.* 工作室

5. (**E**) 這些作品是「由」知名藝術家所創作的，為被動語態，故選 (E) *by*，後接行為者。

6. (**C**) 關係副詞 *where* 表示地點，引導形容詞子句，修飾先行詞 studio。

Artrain doesn't have an engine. Instead, it is [7](B) connected to regular trains and brought from one town to the next. The train's stops are planned carefully, [8](I) with special events and school visits in mind.

　　藝術列車並沒有引擎。相反地，它是和普通火車相連，就這樣被帶往一個接一個的城鎮。列車的停靠站都經過精心策劃，有時也會考慮安排特展和學校訪問。

engine〔'ɛndʒən〕*n.* 引擎
instead〔ɪn'stɛd〕*adv.* 取而代之的是；相反地
regular〔'rɛgjələ〕*adj.* 普通的　　stop〔stɑp〕*n.* 停車站
plan〔plæn〕*v.* 規劃　　*special event* 特展

7. (**B**) 依句意，因為藝術列車沒有引擎，所以是和一般的火車「相連」，才能移動，故選 (B) *connected*〔kə'nɛktɪd〕*v.* 連接。

8. (**I**) 「*with* + *O.* + 補語」表示附帶狀態。
　　with sth. *in mind* 把考慮在內；考慮到

Arranging a traveling show like this is hard work, but local volunteers work with the train staff to help make each stop a [9](J) success.

安排這種巡迴展，可不是一件簡單的事，不過地方上的志工，會和列車上的工作人員共同合作，讓每一站的展覽都很成功。

> arrange〔ə'rendʒ〕v. 安排　　traveling〔'trævlɪŋ〕adj. 巡迴的
> local〔'lokḷ〕adj. 當地的　　volunteer〔,vɑlən'tɪr〕n. 志工
> staff〔stæf〕n. 工作人員

9. (**J**)　依句意，他們要讓每站的展覽都很「成功」，故選 (J) ***success***。

When Artrain arrives in a town, kids and adults line up to see the treasures inside. For many of the youngsters, especially, it is their first visit to an art museum. And when they step down from the last car, their most common [10](A) reaction is "Let's go through again!"

當藝術列車抵達一個城鎮之後，大人和小孩都會排隊來參觀裡面的珍寶。尤其對許多年輕人來說，這是他們第一次參觀美術館。當他們從最後一節車廂下來時，他們最常見的反應就是：「我們再進去一次！」

> ***line up*** 排隊　　treasure〔'trɛʒɚ〕n. 寶藏
> youngster〔'jʌŋstɚ〕n. 青少年
> especially〔ə'spɛʃəlɪ〕adv. 尤其是
> ***step down*** 下來　　common〔'kɑmən〕adj. 常見的

10. (**A**)　依句意，當人們從最後一節車廂走下來時，他們最普遍的「反應」就是：「我們再去看一次！」，故選 (A) ***reaction***〔rɪ'ækʃən〕n. 反應。

TEST 7

說明： 第 1 至 10 題，每題一個空格。請依文意在文章後所提供的 (A) 到 (J) 選項中分別選出最適當者。

In rare instances, societies ___1___ killing. It is accepted in war, in self-defense and, within the United States, for punishment of terrible crimes. This week, the Supreme Court is considering another exception: whether doctors should be allowed to ___2___ the end of life for people who are terminally ill. The issues explored in the court ___3___ the question: Do circumstances ever justify ___4___ doctors from healers into deliverers of death?

Euthanasia originally meant "a gentle and easy death." It has come to mean "a good death of another" or "___5___ killing." Euthanasia is, therefore, a procedure undertaken by a doctor to end the life of a patient who is ___6___ unbearable pain with no medical chance of recovery. In this situation, a patient may ask the doctor to end his or her life.

The crucial issue is whether the essence of life resides in the heart or in the brain. Because the body rarely ___7___ all its systems at once, and because hospitals have access ___8___ the most modern life-preserving machinery, it is entirely possible for the brain, deprived ___9___ an adequate supply of oxygen, to die while the patient, often with the help of hospital equipment, remains alive. To many observers this "brain death" should constitute the legal definition of death because it leaves the patient ___10___ more than a vegetable.

(A) little   (B) transforming   (C) speed

(D) of   (E) center on   (F) shuts down

(G) in   (H) mercy   (I) to

(J) justify

TEST 7 詳解

In rare instances, societies [1](J) justify killing. It is accepted in war, in self-defense and, within the United States, for punishment of terrible crimes. This week, the Supreme Court is considering another exception: whether doctors should be allowed to [2](C) speed the end of life for people who are terminally ill.

在很罕見的情況中，社會會認為殺人是無罪的。在戰爭、正當防衛時，以及在美國境內，要懲罰嚴重的罪行時，殺人是被接受的。在本週，最高法院正在考慮另一個例外：醫生是否應該被允許，加快結束末期病患的生命。

rare〔rɛr〕*adj.* 罕見的

instance〔'ɪnstəns〕*n.* 情況（= *situation*）

accepted〔ək'sɛptɪd〕*adj.* 為一般人所接受的

self-defense〔ˌsɛlfdɪ'fɛns〕*n.* 自衛；正當防衛

within〔wɪð'ɪn, wɪθ'ɪn〕*prep.* 在⋯之內

punishment〔'pʌnɪʃmənt〕*n.* 處罰

terrible〔'tɛrəbļ〕*adj.* 可怕的；嚴重的　　crime〔kraɪm〕*n.* 罪

supreme〔sə'prim〕*adj.* 最高的　　court〔kort〕*n.* 法院

Supreme Court 最高法院　　exception〔ɪk'sɛpʃən〕*n.* 例外

the end of life 死亡（= *death*）

terminally〔'tɜmənļɪ〕*adv.* 末期地

1.(**J**) ***justify***〔'dʒʌstəˌfaɪ〕*v.* 使成為正當；認為～無罪

2.(**C**) ***speed***〔spid〕*v.* 加速

The issues explored in the court ^{3}(E) center on the question: Do circumstances ever justify ^{4}(B) transforming doctors from healers into deliverers of death?

在法院中探討的議題，都是集中於這個問題：在這種情況下，醫生真的可以從醫治者轉變成殺手嗎？

issue〔ˈɪʃjʊ〕 *n.* 議題 　　explore〔ɪkˈsplor〕 *v.* 探討
circumstances〔ˈsɝkəmˌstænsɪz〕 *n. pl.* 情況
ever〔ˈɛvɚ〕 *adv.* 曾經
healer〔ˈhilɚ〕 *n.* 醫治者 　　deliverer〔dɪˈlɪvərɚ〕 *n.* 遞送者
deliverer of death 殺手〔 = *killer* 〕

3. (**E**) *center on* 集中於

4. (**B**) *transform*〔trænsˈfɔrm〕 *v.* 使轉變
   transform A *into* B 把 A 轉變為 B

Euthanasia originally meant "a gentle and easy death." It has come to mean "a good death of another" or "^{5}(H) mercy killing." Euthanasia is, therefore, a procedure undertaken by a doctor to end the life of a patient who is ^{6}(G) in unbearable pain with no medical chance of recovery. In this situation, a patient may ask the doctor to end his or her life.

安樂死原本的意思是「溫和且舒適的死亡」。它的意思後來則演變為「讓別人舒服地死」，或「安樂死」。因此，如果病人承受著無法忍受的疼痛，而且在醫療方面，已經沒有康復的機會，那麼醫生就會採用安樂死的程序，來結束病人的生命。

euthanasia〔͵juθəˈneʒɪə〕*n.* 安樂死

originally〔əˈrɪdʒənlɪ〕*adv.* 原本

gentle〔ˈdʒɛntl̩〕*adj.* 溫和的　　easy〔ˈizɪ〕*adj.* 舒適的

come to 演變爲　　procedure〔prəˈsidʒɚ〕*n.* 程序

undertake〔͵ʌndɚˈtek〕*v.* 採取　　end〔ɛnd〕*v.* 結束

patient〔ˈpeʃənt〕*n.* 病人

unbearable〔ʌnˈbɛrəbl̩〕*adj.* 無法忍受的

medical〔ˈmɛdɪkl̩〕*adj.* 醫療的

recovery〔rɪˈkʌvərɪ〕*n.* 康復

5. (**H**) ***mercy***〔ˈmɜsɪ〕*n.* 慈悲

　　mercy killing 安樂死 (= *euthanasia*)

6. (**G**) ***be in pain*** 處於痛苦之中

The crucial issue is whether the essence of life resides in the heart or in the brain. Because the body rarely [7](**F**) shuts down all its systems at once, and because hospitals have access [8](**I**) to the most modern life-preserving machinery, it is entirely possible for the brain, deprived [9](**D**) of an adequate supply of oxygen, to die while the patient, often with the help of hospital equipment, remains alive.

最重要的問題是，生命的本質是在於心，還是腦。因爲身體的系統，很少會立刻全部停止運作，而且因爲醫院能夠使用最現代化的生命維持裝置，所以，由於腦部缺氧而導致腦死的病人，常因爲有醫院設備的協助，而仍然存活，這是完全有可能的。

crucial (ˈkruʃəl) *adj.* 非常重要的

essence (ˈɛsn̩s) *n.* 本質；要素

reside in 在於 (= *lie in*)　　rarely (ˈrɛrlɪ) *adv.* 很少

at once 立刻　　access (ˈæksɛs) *n.* 使用權

preserve (prɪˈzɝv) *v.* 保存

machinery (məˈʃinərɪ) *n.* 機器；機械裝置

life-preserving machinery 生命維持裝置 (= *life-support system*)

deprive (dɪˈpraɪv) *v.* 剝奪；使喪失

adequate (ˈædəkwɪt) *adj.* 足夠的

supply (səˈplaɪ) *n.* 供給　　oxygen (ˈɑksədʒən) *n.* 氧氣

remain (rɪˈmen) *v.* 仍然　　alive (əˈlaɪv) *adj.* 活著的

7. (**F**) ***shut down*** 停止運轉；停工

8. (**I**) ***have access to*** 有使用～的權利

9. (**D**) ***be deprived of*** 喪失

To many observers this "brain death" should constitute the legal definition of death because it leaves the patient [10](A) little more than a vegetable.

對許多觀察家而言，這種「腦死」的現象，應該可以構成法律上對死亡的定義，因爲它讓病人幾乎就跟植物人差不多。

observer (əbˈzɝvɚ) *n.* 觀察家　　***brain death*** 腦死

constitute (ˈkɑnstəˌtjut) *v.* 構成

legal (ˈligl̩) *adj.* 法律上的　　definition (ˌdɛfəˈnɪʃən) *n.* 定義

leave (liv) *v.* 使處於…狀態　　vegetable (ˈvɛdʒətəbl̩) *n.* 植物人

10. (**A**) ***little more than*** 幾乎就是 (= *almost*)

　　　　cf. no more than 只是 (= *only*)

TEST 8

說明: 第 1 至 10 題，每題一個空格。請依文意在文章後所提供的 (A) 到 (J) 選項中分別選出最適當者。

Do we ___1___ too much? To some people, the answer is evident: If there is only so much food, ___2___, and other materials to go ___3___, the more we use up, the less must be available.

But ___4___ a philosophical level, another response is that a meaningful life is not one devoted to accumulating material possessions. Early preservationists gave moral reasons for protecting the natural world. John Muir, for example, described nature not as a ___5___ but as a companion.

Today, those who want to ___6___ the natural environment offer economic reasons for their policies. They insist we are running out of resources. They say we will suffer from resource ___7___. Although

it seems economic reasons have succeeded better

than moral ones nowadays, there is one point ___8___.

Thoreau said it best: "A man's relation to nature must

come near ___9___ a very personal one." In other

words, although we must use nature, we shall uncover

its true worth — too much consumption makes us

___10___ affection for the natural world.

(A) to   (B) consume   (C) lose

(D) on   (E) around   (F) preserve

(G) commodity   (H) petroleum   (I) scarcity

(J) missing

TEST 8 詳解

Do we ^{1}**(B) consume** too much? To some people, the answer
is evident: If there is only so much food, ^{2}**(H) petroleum**, and other
materials to go ^{3}**(E) around**, the more we use up, the less must be
available.

　　我們是不是消耗太多物資了呢？對某些人而言，答案是顯而易見的：
如果我們只有這麼多的食物、石油以及其他的原料足以分配，我們消耗
得越多，剩下可供使用的一定就會越少。

> evident〔'ɛvədənt〕*adj.* 明顯的
> material〔mə'tɪrɪəl〕*n.* 原料
> **go around** 足夠分配　　 **use up** 用光
> available〔ə'veləbḷ〕*adj.* 可以使用的

1. (**B**) 我們是不是「消耗」太多物資了，與其後片語 use up「用光」
　　相呼應，故選 (B) *consume*〔kən'sum , -'sjum〕*v.* 消耗。

2. (**H**) 「石油」與食物，以及其他的原料，都是人類生存所必須消耗
　　的物資，故選 (H) *petroleum*〔pə'trolɪəm〕*n.* 石油。

3. (**E**) *go around* 足夠分配

But ^{4}**(D) on** a philosophical level, another response is that a
meaningful life is not one devoted to accumulating material
possessions. Early preservationists gave moral reasons for
protecting the natural world. John Muir, for example, described
nature not as a ^{5}**(G) commodity** but as a companion.

　　但是以哲學的標準看來，另一種答案卻是，有意義的生命，並不在於致力累積物質財產。早期的保護主義者則提供一些道德理由，說明我們得保護自然世界。舉例來說，約翰・繆爾就描述自然不是一種商品，而是人類的朋友。

philosophical〔,fɪlə'safɪk!〕*adj.* 哲學的　　level〔'lɛv!〕*n.* 標準
response〔rɪ'spɑns〕*n.* 回答
meaningful〔'minɪŋfəl〕*adj.* 有意義的
devote〔dɪ'vot〕*v.* 貢獻　　accumulate〔ə'kjumjə,let〕*v.* 累積
material〔mə'tɪrɪəl〕*adj.* 物質的
possessions〔pə'zɛʃənz〕*n. pl.* 財產
preservationist〔,prɛzɚ'veʃənɪst〕*n.* 保護（自然環境）主義者
moral〔'mɔrəl〕*adj.* 道德的　　reason〔'rizn̩〕*n.* 理由
protect〔prə'tɛkt〕*v.* 保護　　companion〔kəm'pænjən〕*n.* 朋友

4. (**D**) *on a~level* 以～標準看來

5. (**G**) 自然並非「商品」，而是朋友，選 (G) *commodity*〔kə'mɑdətɪ〕*n.* 商品。

Today, those who want to [6](**F**) preserve the natural environment offer economic reasons for their policies. They insist we are running out of resources. They say we will suffer from resource [7](**I**) scarcity. Although it seems economic reasons have succeeded better than moral ones nowadays, there is one point [8](**J**) missing. Thoreau said it best: "A man's relation to nature must come near [9](**A**) to a very personal one." In other words, although we must use nature, we shall uncover its true worth — too much consumption makes us [10](**C**) lose affection for the natural world.

　　今日，想要保存自然環境的人士，為他們的政策提出經濟上的理由。他們堅稱我們的資源已經快用完了。他們說我們將會因缺乏資源而受害。雖然，今天經濟上的理由，似乎比道德理由更能打動人心，但是有個重點還是被遺漏了。梭羅說得最好：「人和自然之間的關係，必須類似接近於人與人之間的關係。」換句話說，雖然我們一定得使用自然，我們也必須發掘它的真正價值——過多的消耗，會使我們失去對自然世界的感情。

economic〔͵ikə'namɪk〕*adj.* 經濟（上）的
insist〔ɪn'sɪst〕*v.* 堅稱；極力主張　　　***run out of*** 用完
resources〔rɪ'sorsɪz〕*n. pl.* 資源
suffer〔'sʌfə〕*v.*（因…而）受害 < *from* >
succeed〔sək'sid〕*v.* 成功；打動人心
point〔pɔɪnt〕*n.* 重點　　　relation〔rɪ'leʃən〕*n.* 關係
personal〔'pɜsn̩l〕*adj.* 個人的　　　***in other words*** 換句話說
uncover〔ʌn'kʌvə〕*v.* 發掘　　　worth〔wɜθ〕*n.* 價值
consumption〔kən'sʌmpʃən〕*n.* 消耗
affection〔ə'fɛkʃən〕*n.* 感情

6. (**F**) 那些想要「保存」自然環境的人士，提出經濟上的理由，選 (F) ***preserve***〔prɪ'zɜv〕*v.* 保存（自然環境等）。

7. (**I**) 依句意，資源快用完了，我們將會因「缺乏」資源而受害，選 (I) ***scarcity***〔'skɛrsətɪ〕*n.* 缺少。

8. (**J**) 依句意，有個重點「遺漏了」，選 (J) ***missing***。

9. (**A**) ***come near to*** 接近；類似

10. (**C**) 過多的消耗會使我們「失去」對自然世界的感情，選 (C) ***lose***〔luz〕*v.* 失去。

TEST 9

說明： 第 1 至 10 題，每題一個空格。請依文意在文章後所提供的 (A) 到 (J) 選項中分別選出最適當者。

Automobile accidents are as familiar as the common cold but ___1___ more deadly. Yet their cause and control ___2___ a serious problem, difficult to solve.

Experts have long recognized that this problem has multiple causes; ___3___ the very least, it is a "driver-vehicle-roadway" problem. If all drivers ___4___ good judgment at all times, there would be few accidents. But this is rather like saying that if all people were virtuous, there would be no ___5___.

Improved design has helped make highways ___6___ much safer. But the tide of accidents continues to rise because of "man-failure" and an enormous ___7___ in the number of automobiles on the road.

Attention is now ___8___ increasingly to the third member of the accident-triangle — the car ___9___. Assuming that accidents are bound ___10___ occur, people want to know how cars can be built better to protect the occupants.

(A) relatively   (B) remain   (C) increase   (D) exercised
(E) turning   (F) at   (G) to   (H) crime
(I) far   (J) itself

TEST 9 詳解

Automobile accidents are as familiar as the common cold but
[1](I) far more deadly. Yet their cause and control [2](B) remain a
serious problem, difficult to solve.

汽車發生事故和感冒一樣常見，只不過前者致命多了。然而，車禍
的起因和預防，一直是個嚴重的問題，很難解決。

automobile〔ˋɔtəməˏbil〕*n.* 汽車
familiar〔fəˋmɪljɚ〕*adj.* 熟悉的   cold〔kold〕*n.* 感冒
deadly〔ˋdɛdlɪ〕*adj.* 致命的

1. (**I**) *far* 修飾比較級形容詞。

2. (**B**) 本句缺少動詞，依句意，車禍的起因和預防，「仍舊」是個嚴
   重的問題，故選 (B) *remain*。

Experts have long recognized that this problem has multiple
causes; [3](F) at the very least, it is a "driver-vehicle-roadway"
problem. If all drivers [4](D) exercised good judgment at all times,
there would be few accidents. But this is rather like saying that if
all people were virtuous, there would be no [5](H) crime.

專家早就已經承認，造成這個問題的原因很多；至少，車禍的形成
是一個「駕駛人、車輛和道路」的三角難題。假使所有的駕駛人，都能
發揮良好的判斷力，那就幾乎不會有車禍了。可是這樣就好比說，如果
所有的人品德都很好，那就不會有人犯罪，這是不可能的。

expert〔'ɛkspɜt〕*n.* 專家　　recognize〔'rɛkəg,naɪz〕*v.* 承認

multiple〔'mʌltəpl̩〕*adj.* 多樣的　　vehicle〔'viɪkl̩〕*n.* 車輛

roadway〔'rod,we〕*n.* 道路

judgment〔'dʒʌdʒmənt〕*n.* 判斷

at all times　一直　　rather〔'ræðɚ〕*adv.* 有點

virtuous〔'vɜtʃuəs〕*adj.* 有品德的

3. (**F**)　***at*** (***the very***) ***least*** 至少

　　the very 爲加強語氣，修飾最高級形容詞 least。

4. (**D**)　條件子句缺乏動詞，又依句意，每個駕駛人都「發揮」良好的

　　判斷力，故選 (D) ***exercised***。這裡爲「和現在事實相反」的假

　　設語態，故條件子句用過去式。

5. (**H**)　依句意，假如每個人品德都很好，就不會有「犯罪」了，故選

　　(H) ***crime***。crime〔kraɪm〕*n.* 犯罪

Improved design has helped make highways [6](**A**) relatively

much safer.　But the tide of accidents continues to rise because of

"man-failure" and an enormous [7](**C**) increase in the number of

automobiles on the road.

　　公路的設計經過改良後，已經讓公路相對地安全許多。可是，由於

「人爲疏失」和路上汽車數目大量增加，使得車禍事件持續增加。

improved〔ɪm'pruvd〕*adj.* 改良的

design〔dɪ'zaɪn〕*n.* 設計　　highway〔'haɪ,we〕*n.* 公路

tide〔taɪd〕*n.* 潮流　　failure〔'feljɚ〕*n.* 忽略

enormous〔ɪ'nɔrməs〕*adj.* 巨大的

6. (**A**) 這裡需用副詞來修飾後面的 much safer，依句意，改良後的設計，讓公路「相對地」安全多了，故選 (A) *relatively* (ˈrɛlətɪvlɪ) *adv.* 相對地；比較。

7. (**C**) 由前面的 an 可知，此處需要填名詞，依句意，車輛的「增加」導致車禍發生，故選 (C) *increase*。

Attention is now **⁸(E) turning** increasingly to the third member of the accident-triangle — the car **⁹(J) itself**. Assuming that accidents are bound **¹⁰(G) to** occur, people want to know how cars can be built better to protect the occupants.

　　現在大家關注的重點，已經逐漸轉向車禍三要素中的第三個因素 —— 在車輛本身作加強。假如車禍是不可避免的話，人們想知道是否能讓車輛造得更堅固，以保護車主。

　　attention (əˈtɛnʃən) *n.* 注意
　　increasingly (ɪnˈkrisɪŋlɪ) *adv.* 逐漸
　　triangle (ˈtraɪ͵æŋgl̩) *n.* 三角關係
　　assume (əˈsum) *v.* 假定
　　assuming that 假如～（的話）
　　occupant (ˈɑkjəpənt) *n.* 擁有者

8. (**E**) *turn to* 轉向

9. (**J**) 此處用反身代名詞 *itself* 加強語氣，用來強調前面的受詞 car。

10. (**G**) *be bound to* + *V.* 一定

TEST 10

說明：第 1 至 10 題，每題一個空格。請依文意在文章後所提供的 (A) 到 (J) 選項中分別選出最適當者。

In __1__ you hadn't already guessed, it's now official: women __2__ men hands down at remembering a face. Researchers at Halmstad University in Sweden conducted an online __3__ using 1800 participants, each of whom was given eight tasks involving matching a picture of a face __4__ ten similar faces __5__ various conditions — in profile, silhouette or with different facial expressions. The study also found women were __6__ likely to be __7__ by changes in hairstyles or facial expressions. The result is probably a mixture __8__ genetic differences and training. Women may be better at studying faces because they're more likely to be the main center in a family and have __9__ eye contact with children. The findings have implications for recruitment in such industries as security and customs, where facial __10__ is important.

(A) recognition   (B) experiment   (C) beat
(D) under   (E) more   (F) with   (G) of
(H) case   (I) distracted   (J) less

TEST 10 詳解

In [1](**H**) case you hadn't already guessed, it's now official: women [2](**C**) beat men hands down at remembering a face. Researchers at Halmstad University in Sweden conducted an online [3](**B**) experiment using 1800 participants, each of whom was given eight tasks involving matching a picture of a face [4](**F**) with ten similar faces [5](**D**) under various conditions — in profile, silhouette or with different facial expressions.

如果你還沒猜出來的話，現在結果已正式公布了：女性在記得某人的臉孔這方面，輕易地擊敗男性。瑞典漢姆斯達大學的研究人員們，進行一項線上實驗，有一千八百人參與，每位參加者給予八項任務，其中包含要將一張臉孔的照片，與十張在各種狀況下、很相似的臉孔做比對——這些狀況包括側面、側面剪影，或是其他不同的臉部表情。

official〔əˈfɪʃəl〕*adj.* 正式的	*hands down* 輕易地（ = *easily*）
Sweden〔ˈswidn̩〕*n.* 瑞典	conduct〔kənˈdʌkt〕*v.* 進行
online〔ˈɑnˌlaɪn〕*adj.* 線上的	participant〔pɚˈtɪsəpənt〕*n.* 參加者
task〔tæsk〕*n.* 工作；任務	involve〔ɪnˈvɑlv〕*v.* 包含
various〔ˈvɛrɪəs〕*adj.* 各種的	condition〔kənˈdɪʃən〕*n.* 狀況
profile〔ˈprofaɪl〕*n.* 側面	silhouette〔ˌsɪluˈɛt〕*n.* 側面剪影
facial〔ˈfeʃəl〕*adj.* 臉部的	expression〔ɪkˈsprɛʃən〕*n.* 表情

1. (**H**) *in case* 如果，為連接詞，相當於 if 之意。

2. (**C**) 依句意，女性「擊敗」男性，選 (C) *beat*。

3. (**B**) *experiment*〔ɪkˈspɛrəmənt〕*n.* 實驗

4. (**F**) *match* A *with* B 使 A 與 B 配合

5. (**D**) 表示「在～狀況下」，介系詞應用 *under*，選 (D)。

The study also found women were ^{6}(J) less likely to be ^{7}(I) distracted by changes in hairstyles or facial expressions. The result is probably a mixture ^{8}(G) of genetic differences and training. Women may be better at studying faces because they're more likely to be the main center in a family and have ^{9}(E) more eye contact with children. The findings have implications for recruitment in such industries as security and customs, where facial ^{10}(A) recognition is important.

研究中也發現，女性較不可能因髮型或臉部表情改變，而被混淆。這可能是遺傳上的差異，再加上後天訓練，所造成的結果。女性較擅長研究人的臉部表情，因爲她們較可能是一個家庭的重心所在，而且和小孩子有較多的目光接觸。這些研究結果和部分企業，如保全業和海關等單位，會有些關聯，因爲在這些工作中，臉部辨識是很重要的。

be likely to + *V.* 可能　　hairstyle ('hɛr,staɪl) *n.* 髮型
mixture ('mɪkstʃɚ) *n.* 混合　　genetic (dʒə'nɛtɪk) *adj.* 遺傳的
be good at 擅長 (此處用比較級 *be better at*)
eye contact 目光接觸　　findings ('faɪndɪŋz) *n. pl.* 研究結果
implication (,ɪmplɪ'keʃən) *n.* 關聯；暗示
recruitment (rɪ'krutmənt) *n.* 招募新人
industry ('ɪndəstrɪ) *n.* 企業　　security (sɪ'kjurətɪ) *n.* 保全
customs ('kʌstəmz) *n.* 海關

6. (**J**) 依句意應是女性「較不」會被混淆，選 (J) *less*。

7. (**I**) *distract* (dɪ'strækt) *v.* 使分心；使混淆

8. (**G**) 表示「是～的混合」，介系詞應用 *of*，選 (G)。

9. (**E**) 依句意，女性和小孩子有「較多的」目光接觸，選 (E) *more*。

10. (**A**) *recognition* (,rɛkəg'nɪʃən) *n.* 辨認

TEST 11

說明： 第 1 至 10 題，每題一個空格。請依文意在文章後所提供的 (A) 到 (J) 選項中分別選出最適當者。

    Flowers are sunny, positive, and full of ___1___. The sight, the smell, and the touch of them delight me so much. When I look at how flowers blossom and ___2___, I can feel how time goes by, how everything changes. I consider myself pretty lucky to combine my interests with my work, and to do my job in such an ___3___ environment.

    I believe everyone is ___4___ with talents in a certain field. As for me, I am very ___5___ with numbers, but I have always had a keen sense of how flowers can be arranged to look their best. Therefore, when I graduated from the horticulture department of a vocational school, I decided to ___6___ a career that utilized my ability. It took me ten years to

accumulate enough experience, confidence, and

investment __7__ to start my own business.

I opened this flower shop last March, and pay

NT$50,000 for __8__. After one year in operation,

I was able to make ends meet, and began to __9__

investment returns. However, it's __10__ that I

will make big money from such a small shop. But

so far I am happy with my small flower shop.

(A) reap   (B) vitality   (C) unlikely

(D) endowed   (E) agreeable   (F) pursue

(G) awkward   (H) wither   (I) capital

(J) rent

TEST 11 詳解

Flowers are sunny, positive, and full of [1](B) vitality. The sight, the smell, and the touch of them delight me so much. When I look at how flowers blossom and [2](H) wither, I can feel how time goes by, how everything changes. I consider myself pretty lucky to combine my interests with my work, and to do my job in such an [3](E) agreeable environment.

花朵是令人愉快、正面、且充滿活力的。看見它們,聞到它們,觸摸它們,都使我感到非常愉快。當我看到花朵如何開放和凋謝時,我可以感受到時光飛逝,事物變遷。我認為自己非常幸運,可以把興趣和工作相結合,在這麼一個愉快的環境下工作。

sunny ('sʌnɪ) *adj.* 令人愉快的 (= *cheerful*)
positive ('pɑzətɪv) *adj.* 正面的
delight (dɪ'laɪt) *v.* 使高興
blossom ('blɑsəm) *v.* 開花　　*go by*　(時間)消逝
consider (kən'sɪdə) *v.* 認為
combine (kəm'baɪn) *v.* 結合
environment (ɪn'vaɪrənmənt) *n.* 環境

1. (**B**) 花朵充滿「活力」,選 (B) *vitality* (vaɪ'tælətɪ) *n.* 活力。

2. (**H**) 看到花開花「謝」,可以感覺到時間消逝,選 (H) *wither* ('wɪðə) *v.* 凋謝;枯萎。

3. (**E**) 我認為自己很幸運,在這麼「愉快的」環境中工作,選 (E) *agreeable* (ə'griəbḷ) *adj.* (令人)愉快的。

I believe everyone is [4](D) endowed with talents in a certain field. As for me, I am very [5](G) awkward with numbers, but I have always had a keen sense of how flowers can be arranged to look their best. Therefore, when I graduated from the horticulture department of a vocational school, I decided to [6](F) pursue a career that utilized my ability. It took me ten years to accumulate enough experience, confidence, and investment [7](I) capital to start my own business.

　　我相信每一個人在某種領域，一定具有一些才能。至於我，我對數字非常不擅長，但是我對於如何把花插得最好看，一直有敏銳的感覺。因此，當我從職業學校的園藝系畢業時，我決定要從事一個可以利用自我能力的工作。我花了十年的時間，累積足夠的經驗、信心以及投資資金，去開創自己的事業。

　　field〔fild〕 *n.* 領域　　*as for* 至於
　　be awkward with 不擅長
　　keen〔kin〕 *adj.* 敏銳的　　arrange〔ə'rendʒ〕 *v.* 排列
　　horticulture〔'hɔrtɪ,kʌltʃɚ〕 *n.* 園藝
　　department〔dɪ'pɑrtmənt〕 *n.* 科系；部門
　　vocational〔vo'keʃənl̩〕 *adj.* 職業的
　　pursue〔pɚ'su〕 *v.* 追求；從事　　utilize〔'jutl̩,aɪz〕 *v.* 利用
　　accumulate〔ə'kjumjə,let〕 *v.* 累積
　　confidence〔'kɑnfədəns〕 *n.* 信心
　　investment〔ɪn'vɛstmənt〕 *n.* 投資

4. (**D**) *be endowed with* 天生具有　　*endow* 〔 ɪn'dau 〕 *v.* 賦予

5. (**G**) 我對數字「不擅長」，選 (G) *awkward* 〔'ɔkwəd 〕 *adj.* 笨拙的。

6. (**F**) *pursue a career* 「從事一項工作」，選 (F) *career* 〔 kə'rɪr 〕 *n.* 職業。

7. (**I**) 投資需要的是「資金」，故選 (I) *capital* 〔'kæpətḷ 〕 *n.* 資金。

　　I opened this flower shop last March, and pay NT$50,000 for
8(J) rent. After one year in operation, I was able to make ends
meet, and began to **9**(A) reap investment returns. However, it's
10(C) unlikely that I will make big money from such a small shop.
But so far I am happy with my small flower shop.

　　我去年三月開了這家花店，付五萬元的租金。經營一年之後，我能
夠收支平衡，並且開始獲利。然而，對我而言，要從這樣一家小店來賺
大錢是不可能的。但是到目前為止，我對我的小花店非常滿意。

operation 〔ˌɑpə'reʃən 〕 *n.* 營運
make (both) ends meet 收支平衡
return 〔 rɪ'tɝn 〕 *n.* 獲利　　*make big money* 賺大錢
be happy with 對～感到滿意

8. (**J**) 開花店，付五萬元的「租金」，選 (J) *rent* 〔 rɛnt 〕 *n.* 租金。

9. (**A**) 經營一年後，開始「獲」利，選 (A) *reap* 〔 rip 〕 *v.* 收割；獲得。

10. (**C**) 店很小又想賺大錢是「不可能的」，故選 (C) *unlikely*
〔 ʌn'laɪklɪ 〕 *adj.* 不可能的。
注意：unlikely「不可能的」是形容詞，不是副詞。

TEST 12

說明： 第 1 至 10 題，每題一個空格。請依文意在文章後所提供的 (A) 到 (J) 選項中分別選出最適當者。

Although there are some ___1___, frightening aspects of the weather, there is, of course, considerable beauty too. The rainbow is one simple, lovely example of nature's ___2___ mysteries.

You usually can see a rainbow when the sun comes out after a rain shower or in the fine ___3___ of a waterfall or fountain. Although sunlight ___4___ to be white, it actually is made up of a mixture of colors — all the colors in the rainbow. We see a rainbow because thousands of tiny raindrops act as ___5___ and prisms on the sunlight. Prisms are objects ___6___ bend light, splitting it into bands of color.

You will always see morning rainbows in the west, with the sun behind you. Afternoon rainbows, ___7___, are always in the east. To see a rainbow, the sun can be no higher than forty-two degrees — nearly ___8___ up the sky. Sometimes, if the sunlight is strong and the light is ___9___ twice in the water droplets, the color bands are fainter and in reverse ___10___ in the second band.

(A) appears   (B) order   (C) likewise   (D) reflected

(E) that   (F) mist   (G) atmospheric   (H) mirrors

(I) violent   (J) halfway

TEST 12 詳解

Although there are some [1](I) violent, frightening aspects of the weather, there is, of course, considerable beauty too. The rainbow is one simple, lovely example of nature's [2](G) atmospheric mysteries.

天氣雖然有些方面是很劇烈、恐怖的，但是它當然也有不少美麗之處。彩虹就是天氣奧秘中，一個簡單又可愛的典型。

frightening (ˈfraɪtṇɪŋ) *adj.* 恐怖的　　aspect (ˈæspɛkt) *n.* 方面
considerable (kənˈsɪdərəbḷ) *adj.* 相當多的
rainbow (ˈrenˌbo) *n.* 彩虹　　lovely (ˈlʌvlɪ) *adj.* 可愛的
mystery (ˈmɪstrɪ) *n.* 奧秘

1. (**I**) 由後面的 frightening「恐怖的」可知，此處應填一個意義相當的形容詞，故選 (I) *violent* (ˈvaɪələnt) *adj.* 激烈的。

2. (**G**) 彩虹爲大自然的「天氣」奧秘之一，故選 (G) *atmospheric* (ˌætməsˈfɛrɪk) *adj.* 大氣的；天氣的。

You usually can see a rainbow when the sun comes out after a rain shower or in the fine [3](F) mist of a waterfall or fountain. Although sunlight [4](A) appears to be white, it actually is made up of a mixture of colors — all the colors in the rainbow.

你通常會在雨過天晴的時候，或是在瀑布或噴泉的水霧中看到彩虹。雖然陽光看起來是白的，事實上，它是由各種顏色混合而成——就是彩虹的七個顏色。

waterfall (ˈwɔtɚˌfɔl) *n.* 瀑布　　fountain (ˈfauntṇ) *n.* 噴泉
be made up of 由～組成　　mixture (ˈmɪkstʃɚ) *n.* 混合

3. (**F**) 根據句意，我們可以在瀑布或噴泉的「水霧」中，看到彩虹，故選 (F) ***mist*** 〔 mɪst 〕 *n.* 霧；水氣。

4. (**A**) ***appear to V.*** 看起來 (= *seem to V.*)

We see a rainbow because thousands of tiny raindrops act as
[5](**H**) mirrors and prisms on the sunlight. Prisms are objects
[6](**E**) that bend light, splitting it into bands of color.
我們可以看到彩虹，是因為有數以千計的小雨滴，它們就像鏡子和三稜鏡，能折射光線。三稜鏡是可以使光線折射的東西，並把光線分成好幾條色帶。

> tiny 〔'taɪnɪ〕 *adj.* 極小的　　raindrop 〔'ren,drɑp〕 *n.* 雨滴
> ***act as*** 充當　　prism 〔'prɪzəm〕 *n.* 三稜鏡
> object 〔'abdʒɪkt〕 *n.* 東西　　bend 〔 bɛnd 〕 *v.* 使彎曲
> split 〔 splɪt 〕 *v.* 使分裂　　band 〔 bænd 〕 *n.* 帶

5. (**H**) 根據句意，小雨滴就像「鏡子」和三稜鏡，可以折射光線，故選 (H) ***mirrors*** 〔'mɪrəz〕 *n. pl.* 鏡子。

6. (**E**) 關代 ***that*** 引導形容詞子句，修飾先行詞 objects，在形容詞子句中，that 做主詞。

You will always see morning rainbows in the west, with the
sun behind you. Afternoon rainbows, [7](**C**) likewise, are always in
the east. To see a rainbow, the sun can be no higher than forty-two
degrees — nearly [8](**J**) halfway up the sky.

早上背向太陽，你就可以在西邊看到彩虹。同樣地，午後的彩虹總
是出現在東方。如果你想看到彩虹，太陽的高度不能超過四十二度──
必須幾乎是在半空中。

degree (dɪˈgri) *n.* 度

7. (**C**) 由前句可知，只要背向太陽，即可看到彩虹，所以早上會在西
邊看到彩虹，「同樣地」，下午會在東邊，故選 (C) *likewise*
(ˈlaɪk͵waɪz) *adv.* 同樣地。

8. (**J**) 由前句可知，想要看到彩虹，太陽的高度不能超過四十二度，
幾乎是在「半」空中，故選 (J) *halfway* (ˈhæfˈwe) *adv.* 在中
途；到一半。

Sometimes, if the sunlight is strong and the light is [9]**(D) reflected**
twice in the water droplets, the color bands are fainter and in
reverse [10]**(B) order** in the second band.

有時如果陽光過強，使得光線在水滴裡折射兩次時，第二道彩虹的色帶
會比較淺，而且排列順序會顛倒。

droplet (ˈdrɑplɪt) *n.* 小水滴
faint (fent) *adj.* 微弱的　　reverse (rɪˈvɜs) *adj.* 顛倒的

9. (**D**) 依句意，光線應是在小水滴裡，被「反射」兩次，故選
(D) *reflected* (rɪˈflɛktɪd) *v.* 反射。

10. (**B**) 依句意，第二道彩虹的顏色排列「順序」是顛倒的，故選
(B) *order* (ˈɔrdə) *n.* 順序
in reverse order 順序顛倒的

TEST 13

說明：第 1 至 10 題，每題一個空格。請依文意在文章後所提供的 (A) 到
(J) 選項中分別選出最適當者。

Taiwan, our homeland, ____1____ be called Formosa, meaning
the beautiful island. But unfortunately, the environment is
drastically deteriorating ____2____ deforestation and garbage. Each
year over 24,000 tons of garbage is collected. Where does all this
garbage go? Only a few cities have incinerators to burn up the
____3____ garbage. Much of it is still buried under the ground in
landfills. But the landfills are quickly ____4____, and it's difficult to
build new ones not only because there is not enough land but also
because villagers living near the planned landfills often ____5____
strong protests. So what can we do to solve the garbage problem?

One answer is to urge people to reduce the ____6____ of garbage.
If possible, we should refrain from using ____7____ diapers, dishes,
boxes, etc. They form a large ____8____ of the garbage. Another
answer is to recycle the garbage. Plastic bottles, cans, old
newspapers and clothes should be put in different recycling ____9____
so that they can be reused. ____10____, the importance of recycling
cannot be overemphasized and the general public must
understand it.

(A) disposable   (B) proportion   (C) In a word
(D) filling up   (E) inflammable   (F) volume
(G) as a result of (H) make   (I) used to   (J) containers

TEST 13 詳解

Taiwan, our homeland, ^{1}(I) used to be called Formosa, meaning the beautiful island. But unfortunately, the environment is drastically deteriorating ^{2}(G) as a result of deforestation and garbage.

我們的祖國台灣，以前被稱為福爾摩莎，意思就是漂亮的島。但遺憾的是，由於砍伐森林及垃圾問題，使得環境大為惡化。

> homeland〔'hom,lænd〕 *n.* 祖國
> Formosa〔fɔr'mosə〕 *n.* 福爾摩莎；台灣
> mean〔min〕 *v.* 意思是　　island〔'aɪlənd〕 *n.* 島
> unfortunately〔ʌn'fɔrtʃənɪtlɪ〕 *adv.* 遺憾地
> environment〔ɪn'vaɪrənmənt〕 *n.* 環境
> drastically〔'dræstɪkḷɪ〕 *adv.* 大大地
> deteriorate〔dɪ'tɪrɪə,ret〕 *v.* 惡化
> deforestation〔,difɔrɪs'teʃən〕 *n.* 砍伐森林
> garbage〔'gɑrbɪdʒ〕 *n.* 垃圾

1. (I) *used to* + *V.* 以前

2. (G) *as a result of* 由於 (= *because of*)

Each year over 24,000 tons of garbage is collected. Where does all this garbage go? Only a few cities have incinerators to burn up the ^{3}(E) inflammable garbage. Much of it is still buried under the ground in landfills. But the landfills are quickly ^{4}(D) filling up, and it's difficult to build new ones not only because there is not enough land but also because villagers living near the planned landfills often ^{5}(H) make strong protests. So what can we do to solve the garbage problem?

每一年收集到的垃圾，超過兩萬四千公噸。這些垃圾全都到哪裡去了？只有一些都市有焚化爐，可以用來燒掉可燃的垃圾。許多垃圾仍然被埋在掩埋場的地底下。但是掩埋場很快就要被填滿了，而且很難建造新的，不僅是因爲沒有足夠的土地，而且也是因爲住在掩埋場預定地附近的村民，常會提出強烈的抗議。所以我們該怎麼做，才能解決垃圾問題呢？

ton〔tʌn〕*n.* 公噸　　incinerator〔ɪn'sɪnə,retə〕*n.* 焚化爐

burn up 燒掉　　bury〔'bɛrɪ〕*v.* 掩埋

landfill〔'lænd,fɪl〕*n.* 垃圾掩埋場

not only…but also~ 不僅…而且~

villager〔'vɪlɪdʒə〕*n.* 村民　　planned〔plænd〕*adj.* 預定的

protest〔'protɛst〕*n.* 抗議　　solve〔sɑlv〕*v.* 解決

3. (**E**)　燒掉「可燃的」垃圾，選 (E) ***inflammable***〔ɪn'flæməb!〕*adj.* 可燃的。

4. (**D**)　***fill up*** 被填滿

5. (**H**)　***make strong protests*** 提出強烈的抗議

One answer is to urge people to reduce the [6](**F**) volume of garbage. If possible, we should refrain from using [7](**A**) disposable diapers, dishes, boxes, etc. They form a large [8](**B**) proportion of the garbage.

其中一個解決辦法，就是要呼籲民眾，減少垃圾量。如果可能，我們應該克制自己，不要使用用完即丟的尿布、餐具、盒子等。這些用品構成了大部份的垃圾。

answer〔'ænsə〕*n.* 答案；解決辦法　　urge〔ɝdʒ〕*v.* 呼籲

reduce〔rɪ'djus〕*v.* 減少　　***refrain from*** 克制自己不要

diaper〔'daɪəpə〕*n.* 尿布　　dishes〔'dɪʃɪz〕*n. pl.* 餐具

etc.〔ɛt'sɛtərə〕等等　　form〔fɔrm〕*v.* 構成

6. (**F**) ***volume***〔'vɑljəm〕 *n.* 量

7. (**A**) ***disposable*** 〔 dɪs'pozəbḷ 〕 *adj.* 用完即丟的；免洗的

8. (**B**) ***proportion*** 〔 prə'porʃən 〕 *n.* 比例；部份

Another answer is to recycle the garbage. Plastic bottles, cans, old newspapers and clothes should be put in different recycling [9](J) containers so that they can be reused. [10](C) In a word, the importance of recycling cannot be overemphasized and the general public must understand it.

另一個解決辦法，就是回收垃圾。塑膠瓶、罐子、舊報紙和衣服，應該被放在不同的回收容器中，以便於再利用。總之，回收的重要性，再怎麼強調也不為過，一般大眾必須要了解這一點。

> recycle〔 ri'saɪkḷ 〕 *v.* 回收
> plastic〔'plæstɪk 〕 *adj.* 塑膠的
> bottle〔'bɑtḷ 〕 *n.* 瓶子　　can〔 kæn 〕 *n.* 罐子
> clothes〔 kloðz 〕 *n. pl.* 衣服　　different〔'dɪfərənt 〕 *adj.* 不同的
> recycling〔ˌri'saɪklɪŋ 〕 *n.* 回收　　reuse〔 ri'juz 〕 *v.* 再使用
> overemphasize〔ˌovə'ɛmfəˌsaɪz 〕 *v.* 過分強調
> ***cannot be overemphasized*** 再怎麼強調也不為過
> general〔'dʒɛnərəl 〕 *adj.* 一般的　　***the general public*** 一般民眾

9. (**J**) ***containers*** 〔 kən'tenəz 〕 *n. pl.* 容器

10. (**C**) ***in a word*** 總之

TEST 14

說明： 第 1 至 10 題，每題一個空格。請依文意在文章後所提供的 (A) 到
　　　(J) 選項中分別選出最適當者。

We all know that history, by definition, is ____1____ the past.
But we also know that history, by definition, ____2____ the present.
Whether we write about the past, read about the past, or find out
about it by watching television, we can never ____3____ from the
constraints and concerns of the world in which we ourselves
actually live. It's because we are caught up in the present that
historical writing is not just about the time of which we write,
but also reflects the values, preoccupations and characteristics
____4____ the time in which we write.

History, ____5____ that extent, is not simply something which
is over, dead, gone, and ____6____ : it is a continuing dialog between
the past and the present. In the words of one of the oldest clichés
in the profession, all history is ____7____ this sense contemporary
history. As ____8____ on the past, historians may be the lords of
time, but as ____9____ of the present, we are also, like everyone else,
its victims and its prisoners. In this respect, the study of the
past is a present-minded ____10____ .

(A) endeavor　　(B) escape　　(C) residents　　(D) about

(E) in　　　　　(F) vanished　　(G) to　　　　　(H) of

(I) mirrors　　(J) experts

TEST 14 詳解

We all know that history, by definition, is **[1](D) about** the past. But we also know that history, by definition, **[2](I) mirrors** the present. Whether we write about the past, read about the past, or find out about it by watching television, we can never **[3](B) escape** from the constraints and concerns of the world in which we ourselves actually live.

我們都知道，根據定義，歷史就是有關過去的事。但我們也知道，按照定義，歷史可以反映現在。無論我們寫有關歷史的事、閱讀有關歷史的事，或藉由看電視，發現有關歷史的事，我們都無法逃離，我們眞正居住的這個世界裡，所有的束縛和關切的事。

> definition (ˌdɛfə'nɪʃən) *n.* 定義
> ***by definition*** 根據定義；按照定義　　past (pæst) *n.* 過去
> present ('prɛznt) *n.* 現在　*adj.* 現在的
> constraint (kən'strent) *n.* 壓迫；束縛
> concern (kən'sɜn) *n.* 關心的事

1. (**D**) 歷史是「有關」過去的事，選 (D) ***about***。

2. (**I**) ***mirror*** ('mɪrə) *v.* 反映 (= *reflect*)

3. (**B**) ***escape*** (ə'skep) *v.* 逃離 < *from* >

It's because we are caught up in the present that historical writing is not just about the time of which we write, but also reflects the values, preoccupations and characteristics **[4](H) of** the time in which we write.

就是因爲我們受困於現在，所以歷史的寫作，不僅是有關我們所書寫的
過去，也反映出我們所處的現在，所擁有的價值觀、專注的事情及特色。

> ***be caught up in*** 被困在
> historical〔hɪs'tɔrɪkl〕*adj.* 有關歷史的
> ***not just*** A ***but also*** B 不僅 A，而且 B（ = *not only A but also B* ）
> ***write of*** 寫有關～的事　　reflect〔rɪ'flɛkt〕*v.* 反映
> values〔'væljʊz〕*n. pl.* 價值觀
> preoccupation〔pri,ɑkjə'pɛʃən〕*n.* 專注、熱中的事情
> characteristic〔,kærɪktə'rɪstɪk〕*n.* 特色

4. (**H**) 依句意，歷史也反映出現代「的」價值觀、特色等，在此爲所
　　　　　有格用法，介系詞用 ***of***，選 (H)。

History, [5](G) to that extent, is not simply something which is
over, dead, gone, and [6](F) vanished: it is a continuing dialog
between the past and the present. In the words of one of the
oldest clichés in the profession, all history is [7](E) in this sense
contemporary history.

　　就此程度而言，歷史不只是已結束、已死掉、已消失的事情而已：
它是過去和現在之間，持續的對話。在歷史學家這一行裡，最古老的
陳腔濫調之一就是，所有的歷史，就其意義而言，都算是現代史。

> extent〔ɪk'stɛnt〕*n.* 程度　　continuing〔kən'tɪnjʊɪŋ〕*adj.* 持續的
> dialog〔'daɪə,lɔg〕*n.* 對話（ = *dialogue* ）
> cliché〔kli'ʃe〕*n.* 陳腔濫調
> profession〔prə'fɛʃən〕*n.* 職業（在此指歷史學家）
> contemporary〔kən'tɛmpə,rɛrɪ〕*adj.* 當代的；現代的

5. (**G**) 表示「到達某種程度」，介系詞應用 *to*，選 (G)。

6. (**F**) 依句意，歷史不只是已結束、已死掉、「已消失的」事情而已，
選 (F) *vanished* (ˋvænɪʃt) *adj.* 已消失的。

7. (**E**) sense 在此作「意義」解，指「就～意義」，介系詞用 *in*，
選 (E)。

As [8](J) experts on the past, historians may be the lords of time, but
as [9](C) residents of the present, we are also, like everyone else, its
victims and its prisoners. In this respect, the study of the past is a
present-minded [10](A) endeavor.

身為關於過去的專家，歷史學家可能是時間的主人，但身為現在的居民，
我們也和其他人一樣，是現在的受害者和囚犯。在這個方面，努力研究過
去也是非常具有現代觀的作法。

> historian (hɪsˋtɔrɪən) *n.* 歷史學家　　lord (lɔrd) *n.* 主人
> victim (ˋvɪktɪm) *n.* 受害者　　prisoner (ˋprɪznə) *n.* 囚犯
> respect (rɪˋspɛkt) *n.* 方面 (= *way* ; *sense*)
> present-minded (ˋprɛzn̩tˋmaɪndɪd) *adj.* 有現代觀的

8. (**J**) 歷史學家是關於過去的「專家」，選 (J) *experts* (ˋɛkspɝts) *n. pl.*
專家。

9. (**C**) 我們身為現在的「居民」，選 (C) *residents* (ˋrɛzədənts) *n. pl.*
居民。

10. (**A**) *endeavor* (ɪnˋdɛvə) *n.* 努力

TEST 15

說明： 第 1 至 10 題，每題一個空格。請依文意在文章後所提供的 (A) 到
(J) 選項中分別選出最適當者。

Sandcastles have become big! Once just something
children ___1___ at the beach, sand sculpture now means big
contests and big business.

Businesses that want to ___2___ attention hire professional
sand sculptors to create in sand everything ___3___ automobiles
to skyscrapers. These professionals no ___4___ even need a
beach — they supply their own sand! Once all you needed to
build a sandcastle was your own hands. Nowadays, however,
equipment ___5___ from buckets and shovels to tractors and
jackhammers. As for the contests, at the most important ___6___,
such as the world championship in British Columbia, Canada,
no fewer ___7___ 200,000 people come to be captivated by
teams of sand sculptors working against time ___8___ fun and
prizes. In the end, though, today's super sandcastles suffer the
same ___9___ as any five-year-old's castle. They're all washed
___10___ by the waves!

(A) than   (B) capture   (C) away   (D) longer

(E) ranges   (F) from   (G) fate   (H) built

(I) for   (J) ones

TEST 15 詳解

Sandcastles have become big! Once just something children
¹(H) built at the beach, sand sculpture now means big contests and
big business.

沙堡變大了！以往沙雕只是小孩子在沙灘上所堆出的玩意兒，現在的
沙雕卻代表大型競賽和龐大的商機。

> sandcastle (ˈsændˌkæsl̩) *n.* 沙堡
> sculpture (ˈskʌlptʃɚ) *n.* 雕刻
> **sand sculpture** 沙雕　　contest (ˈkɑntɛst) *n.* 競賽
> business (ˈbɪznɪs) *n.* 生意

1. (**H**) 沙雕為小孩子在沙灘上所「蓋」的東西，故選 (H) **built**。在此
children…beach 為形容詞子句，修飾先行詞 something。

Businesses that want to **²(B) capture** attention hire professional
sand sculptors to create in sand everything **³(F) from** automobiles
to skyscrapers.

想要引人注意的企業，會僱用專業的沙雕家，用沙來創作出任何東
西，從汽車到摩天樓都可以。

> attention (əˈtɛnʃən) *n.* 注意　　hire (haɪr) *v.* 僱用
> professional (prəˈfɛʃənl̩) *adj.* 職業的　　*n.* 專家
> sculptor (ˈskʌlptɚ) *n.* 雕刻家　　**sand sculptor** 沙雕家
> automobile (ˈɔtəməˌbil) *n.* 汽車
> skyscraper (ˈskaɪˌskrepɚ) *n.* 摩天樓

2. (**B**) *capture attention* 引起注意 (= *attract/draw attention*)

capture〔'kæptʃə〕*v.* 引起

3. (**F**) *from* A *to* B 從 A 到 B

These professionals no **4(D) longer** even need a beach — they supply their own sand! Once all you needed to build a sandcastle was your own hands. Nowadays, however, equipment **5(E) ranges** from buckets and shovels to tractors and jackhammers.

而這些沙雕大師，甚至不再需要海灘來創作—他們自己就有沙！以前你要堆沙堡，只靠自己的一雙手。然而現在，從水桶、鏟子到牽引機、輕型鑿岩機，各種器具應有盡有。

supply〔sə'plaɪ〕*v.* 提供
equipment〔ɪ'kwɪpmənt〕*n.* 裝置
bucket〔'bʌkɪt〕*n.* 水桶　　shovel〔'ʃʌvl̩〕*n.* 鏟子
tractor〔'træktə〕*n.* 牽引機
jackhammer〔'dʒæk,hæmə〕*n.* 輕型鑿岩機

4. (**D**) *no longer* 不再

5. (**E**) *range from* A *to* B （範圍）從 A 到 B 都有

As for the contests, at the most important **6(J) ones**, such as the world championship in British Columbia, Canada, no fewer **7(A) than** 200,000 people come to be captivated by teams of sand sculptors working against time **8(I) for** fun and prizes.

說到比賽，在一些重量級的沙雕賽中，例如在加拿大英屬哥倫比亞省所舉辦的世界冠軍沙雕賽裡，多達二十萬的民眾前來參與這場沙雕盛事，各個參與沙雕賽的團隊，為了樂趣和獎品與時間競賽，民眾都為他們的表現深深著迷。

> *as for* 說到；至於
> championship〔'tʃæmpɪənˌʃɪp〕*n.* 冠軍賽
> *British Columbia* 英屬哥倫比亞
> captivate〔'kæptəˌvet〕*v.* 使著迷
> against〔ə'gɛnst〕*prep.* 對抗　　prize〔praɪz〕*n.* 獎品

6. (**J**)　不定代名詞 *ones*，代替前面已經說過的名詞，這裡代替
　　　　 contests。

7. (**A**)　*no fewer than* 多達

8. (**I**)　選手來參加比賽，是「為了」興趣和獎品，故選 (I) *for*。

In the end, though, today's super sandcastles suffer the same
^{9}(G) fate as any five-year-old's castle. They're all washed ^{10}(C) away
by the waves!

然而比賽到最後，當天冠軍沙堡的命運，就和其他五歲小孩所堆的沙堡一樣，它們全都會被海浪給沖走！

> *in the end* 最後　　though〔θo〕*adv.* 然而
> suffer〔'sʌfə〕*v.* 遭遇　　wave〔wev〕*n.* 海浪

9. (**G**)　依句意，比賽冠軍的沙堡和一般沙堡一樣，最後都會被海浪沖
　　　　 走，它們「命運」相同，故選 (G) *fate*〔fet〕*n.* 命運。

10. (**C**)　*wash away* 沖走

TEST 16

說明: 第 1 至 10 題,每題一個空格。請依文意在文章後所提供的 (A) 到
(J) 選項中分別選出最適當者。

Not all ___1___ discoveries are made in laboratories. Some
occur in the most unlikely places. Here is an example. While
walking through a Paris street, Dr. Rene Laënnec saw some
children ___2___ play. He noticed that one child was ___3___ his
ear with his hand on an old wooden plank. Another child at the
other ___4___ of the plank was tapping a message to him on the
wood. Dr. Laënnec had had trouble that ___5___ morning, when
he was trying to hear the heartbeat of a ___6___ patient with his
ear. In the children's game he at once recognized the principle
of the stethoscope, the ___7___ for checking a patient's heartbeat
which is widely used by doctors nowadays.

Dr. Laënnec rushed home and built the first crude stethoscope
from a long and thin ___8___ tube. Then he hurried back to the
hospital to try it ___9___ one of his patients. It ___10___. He
was able to hear the patient's heartbeat with this tube.

(A) at   (B) end   (C) on   (D) worked
(E) fat   (F) device   (G) hollow   (H) chance
(I) very   (J) cupping

TEST 16 詳解

Not all ¹**(H) chance** discoveries are made in laboratories. Some occur in the most unlikely places. Here is an example. While walking through a Paris street, Dr. Rene Laënnec saw some children ²**(A) at** play. He noticed that one child was ³**(J) cupping** his ear with his hand on an old wooden plank. Another child at the other ⁴**(B) end** of the plank was tapping a message to him on the wood.

並非所有偶然的發現，都是出現在實驗室裡。有些是出現在最不可能的地方。以下就是一個例子。當拉埃內克醫生走在巴黎的街頭時，他看到一些小孩正在玩。他注意到有個小孩，用手將耳朵彎成杯狀，將耳朵靠在一塊舊的木板上。在木板另一端的另一個小孩，在木頭上輕輕敲出，要傳給他的訊息。

> laboratory〔'læbrə,torɪ〕*n.* 實驗室
> unlikely〔ʌn'laɪklɪ〕*adj.* 不可能的　　notice〔'notɪs〕*v.* 注意到
> wooden〔'wʊdn̩〕*adj.* 木頭的　　plank〔plæŋk〕*n.* 厚板
> tap〔tæp〕*v.* 輕敲　　wood〔wʊd〕*n.* 木頭

1. (**H**) 依句意，選 (H) *chance*〔tʃæns〕*adj.* 偶然的。

2. (**A**) *at play* 正在玩

3. (**J**) 依句意爲過去進行式，故選 (J) *cupping*。
　　　cup〔kʌp〕*v.* 使彎成杯狀

4. (**B**) *end*〔ɛnd〕*n.* 一端

Dr. Laënnec had had trouble that ⁵**(I) very** morning, when he was trying to hear the heartbeat of a ⁶**(E) fat** patient with his ear. In the children's game he at once recognized the principle of the stethoscope, the ⁷**(F) device** for checking a patient's heartbeat which is widely used by doctors nowadays.

就在當天早上，拉埃內克醫生遇到了一個難題，當時他正想要用耳朵，聽一位肥胖病人的心跳。從那些孩子的遊戲中，他立刻明白聽診器的原理，聽診器就是現在被醫生廣爲使用，以檢查病人心跳的儀器。

> heartbeat〔'hɑrt,bit〕*n.* 心跳　　patient〔'peʃənt〕*n.* 病人
> ***at once*** 立刻　　recognize〔'rɛkəg,naɪz〕*v.* 明白
> principle〔'prɪnsəpl〕*n.* 原理
> stethoscope〔'stɛθə,skop〕*n.* 聽診器
> widely〔'waɪdlɪ〕*adv.* 廣泛地　　nowadays〔'nɑuə,dez〕*adv.* 現今

5. (**I**) ***very*** 可加強名詞語氣，表「正是；就在」。

6. (**E**) 依句意，選 (E) ***fat***〔fæt〕*adj.* 肥胖的。

7. (**F**) ***device***〔dɪ'vaɪs〕*n.* 儀器；裝置

Dr. Laënnec rushed home and built the first crude stethoscope from a long and thin [8](**G**) hollow tube. Then he hurried back to the hospital to try it [9](**C**) on one of his patients. It [10](**D**) worked. He was able to hear the patient's heartbeat with this tube.

拉埃內克醫生趕忙回家，用細長的中空管子，製作出第一個簡陋的聽診器。然後他又匆忙回到醫院，在病人身上試驗。結果眞的行得通。他能夠用這根管子，聽到病人的心跳。

> ***rush home*** 匆忙回家　　build〔bɪld〕*v.* 製作
> crude〔krud〕*adj.* 簡陋的
> from〔frɑm〕*prep.*（表原料）由…製成　　thin〔θɪn〕*adj.* 細的
> tube〔tjub〕*n.* 管子　　hurry〔'hɝɪ〕*v.* 匆忙行進

8. (**G**) ***hollow***〔'hɑlo〕*adj.* 中空的

9. (**C**) ***try sth. on sb.*** 在某人身上試驗某物

10. (**D**) ***work***〔wɝk〕*v.* 有效；行得通

TEST 17

說明： 第 1 至 10 題，每題一個空格。請依文意在文章後所提供的 (A) 到
(J) 選項中分別選出最適當者。

It used to be that the Internet was seen mostly as
a tool for doing research. But these days, the Internet
is as much about entertainment as ___1___ information.
What's more, one of the most popular forms of
entertainment outside the Internet is fast becoming an
___2___ favorite as well. It's the comic strip. You can
find almost any comic strip ___3___ on the Internet.
Many of the famous ones can be found on the websites
of the particular cartoonist's media company. Others
appear on the websites of the newspapers in ___4___
the strips appear.

Of course, the major comic strips are not the only
ones you can find on the Web. Since almost anyone
can ___5___ comics on the Internet, you can find strips
on almost any subject, ranging from the hilarious
___6___ the horrible. The quality of the comics may

be uneven, ___7___ the great variety means there's
sure to be ___8___ one that will make you laugh.
Some sites offer animated comic strips that ___9___
the unique features of the Internet. Others let users
create their own personalized comic pages ___10___
choosing the comics that they want and arranging
them on the page. So if you need some laughs, look
no further than the Internet.

(A) at least   (B) distribute   (C) online
(D) which   (E) take advantage of   (F) by
(G) about   (H) yet   (I) to
(J) imaginable

TEST 17 詳解

It used to be that the Internet was seen mostly as a tool for doing research. But these days, the Internet is as much about entertainment as [1](G) about information. What's more, one of the most popular forms of entertainment outside the Internet is fast becoming an [2](C) online favorite as well. It's the comic strip.

網際網路以前大多被視為是做研究的工具。但是最近,網路既可以獲得資訊,也同樣有娛樂的效果。此外,有一種原本不在網路上的非常受歡迎的娛樂,現在也正快速地,成為網路上最受人喜愛的娛樂形式。那就是漫畫。

> ***used to V.*** 以前　　Internet ('ɪntɚ,nɛt) *n.* 網際網路
> ***be seen as*** 被視為　　mostly ('mostlɪ) *adv.* 大多
> research ('risɝtʃ) *n.* 研究　　***these days*** 最近
> entertainment (,ɛntɚ'tenmənt) *n.* 娛樂
> information (,ɪnfɚ'meʃən) *n.* 資訊　　***what's more*** 此外
> form (fɔrm) *n.* 形式　　outside (aʊt'saɪd) *prep.* 在⋯範圍之外
> favorite ('fevərɪt) *n.* 最喜愛的人或物
> ***as well*** 也 (= *too*)　　***comic strip*** 漫畫

1. (**G**) as⋯as~「和~一樣⋯」為相關對等連接詞,其前後所連接的
   單字或片語,文法地位須相同,前面是介系詞 ***about***,故選 (G)。

2. (**C**) ***online*** ('ɑn,laɪn) *adj.* 線上的;網路上的 (= *on-line*)

You can find almost any comic strip [3](J) imaginable on the Internet. Many of the famous ones can be found on the websites of the particular cartoonist's media company. Others appear on the websites of the newspapers in [4](D) which the strips appear.

在網路上，你幾乎可以找到，任何你想像得到的漫畫。許多有名的漫畫，可以在特定漫畫家的傳媒公司的網站上找到。有些則是出現在，刊登該漫畫的報紙的網站上。

famous〔'feməs〕*adj.* 有名的　　website〔'wɛb,saɪt〕*n.* 網站
particular〔pə'tɪkjələ〕*adj.* 特定的
cartoonist〔kɑr'tunɪst〕*n.* 漫畫家　　***media company*** 傳媒公司
appear〔ə'pɪr〕*v.* 出現　　strip〔strɪp〕*n.* 漫畫（= *comic strip*）

3. (**J**) ***imaginable***〔ɪ'mædʒɪnəbḷ〕*adj.* 想像得到的

4. (**D**) 關代 ***which*** 代替先行詞 newspapers，做介系詞 in 的受詞。

Of course, the major comic strips are not the only ones you can find on the Web. Since almost anyone can **⁵(B) distribute** comics on the Internet, you can find strips on almost any subject, ranging from the hilarious **⁶(I) to** the horrible. The quality of the comics may be uneven, **⁷(H) yet** the great variety means there's sure to be **⁸(A) at least** one that will make you laugh.

當然，在網路上可以找到的，不只是一流的漫畫。由於幾乎任何人都可以將漫畫放到網路上去，所以你幾乎可以找到任何主題的漫畫，從很有趣的，到可怕的都有。漫畫的品質可能良莠不齊，但是種類的多樣性，就表示一定至少會有一則漫畫，是能讓你哈哈大笑的。

major〔'medʒə〕*adj.* 一流的
the Web 網路（= *the Internet* = *the Net*）
comics〔'kɑmɪks〕*n. pl.* 漫畫　　subject〔'sʌbdʒɪkt〕*n.* 主題
hilarious〔hə'lɛrɪəs〕*adj.* 很有趣的
horrible〔'hɔrəbḷ〕*adj.* 可怕的　　quality〔'kwɑlətɪ〕*n.* 品質
uneven〔ʌn'ivən〕*adj.* 不平均的
variety〔və'raɪətɪ〕*n.* 多樣性

5. (**B**) ***distribute*** (dɪ'strɪbjut) *v.* 分發 (= *give out*)

【「把資料放到網路上」的説法有：put/post/distribute/give out *sth.* on the Internet】

6. (**I**) ***range from*** A *to* B （範圍）從 A 到 B 都有

7. (**H**) ***yet*** (jɛt) *conj.* 但是

8. (**A**) ***at least*** 至少

Some sites offer animated comic strips that [9](E) take advantage of the unique features of the Internet. Others let users create their own personalized comic pages [10](F) by choosing the comics that they want and arranging them on the page. So if you need some laughs, look no further than the Internet.

有些網站會利用網路獨特的特性，提供會動的漫畫。有些則是讓使用者，能藉由選擇自己想要的漫畫，在頁面上排列，創造出個人化的漫畫網頁。所以，如果你需要一些笑料，只要上網去看就夠了。

> site (saɪt) *n.* 網站 (= *website*)
> animated ('ænə,metɪd) *adj.* 會動的
> unique (ju'nik) *adj.* 獨特的   feature ('fitʃɚ) *n.* 特性
> personalized ('pɜsnḷ,aɪzd) *adj.* 個人化的
> comic ('kɑmɪk) *adj.* 漫畫的   page (pedʒ) *n.* 頁面
> arrange (ə'rendʒ) *v.* 排列   laugh (læf) *n.* 笑料
> ***look no further than*** 只要看～就夠了 (= *look in no other place than*)

9. (**E**) ***take advantage of*** 利用

10. (**F**) 表「藉由～方法」，介系詞用 ***by***。

TEST 18

說明： 第 1 至 10 題，每題一個空格。請依文意在文章後所提供的 (A) 到
(J) 選項中分別選出最適當者。

    Geologists use an instrument called a seismograph to record
earthquakes and volcanic activity. The seismograph has an ink
pen on it ____1____ is attached to a long arm. The arm is weighted
down, and attached to a spring, which ____2____ the arm to bounce
when the instrument is ____3____. When an earthquake occurs or
a volcano rumbles, the arm bounces, and the pen moves up and
down, ____4____ marks on a piece of paper. The stronger the
movement of the earth, the more the pen moves.

    When an earthquake ____5____ occur, geologists measure the
height of the pen marks to ____6____ how strong it was. A number
from one to nine is assigned to each quake, ____7____ its strength:
nine indicates the strongest quake, and one, the weakest. The
scale is so designed that each number indicates a quake ten times
____8____ powerful than the previous number. An earthquake that
____9____ seven or above is considered a major earthquake. The
scale of numbers is called the Richter scale ____10____ Charles
Richter, the scientist who invented this method of measuring
earthquakes.

(A) after   (B) causes   (C) depending on (D) does
(E) disturbed (F) figure out (G) leaving   (H) measures
(I) more   (J) that

TEST 18 詳解

Geologists use an instrument called a seismograph to record earthquakes and volcanic activity. The seismograph has an ink pen on it **[1](J) that** is attached to a long arm. The arm is weighted down, and attached to a spring, which **[2](B) causes** the arm to bounce when the instrument is **[3](E) disturbed**.

地質學家會使用一種叫做地震儀的儀器，來記錄地震及火山的活動。地震儀上有一支墨水筆，連在長長的臂狀物之上。臂狀物被施以重壓，因而往下垂，臂狀物是連在一個彈簧上，當儀器受到震動，彈簧就會使臂狀物上下移動。

geologist〔dʒɪˈɑlədʒɪst〕*n.* 地質學家
instrument〔ˈɪnstrəmənt〕*n.* 儀器
seismograph〔ˈsaɪsməˌgræf〕*n.* 地震儀　　record〔rɪˈkɔrd〕*v.* 記錄
earthquake〔ˈɜθˌkwek〕*n.* 地震　　volcanic〔vɑlˈkænɪk〕*adj.* 火山的
ink〔ɪŋk〕*n.* 墨水　　attached〔əˈtætʃt〕*adj.* 連接的
arm〔ɑrm〕*n.* 臂狀物　　weight〔wet〕*v.* 施以重壓
spring〔sprɪŋ〕*n.* 彈簧　　bounce〔baʊns〕*v.* 反彈；上上下下

1. (**J**) 關代 *that* 引導形容詞子句，修飾先行詞 pen。

2. (**B**) 依句意，選 (B) *causes*「使」。

3. (**E**) 當這個儀器「被動到、受到干擾」，選 (E) *disturbed*。

When an earthquake occurs or a volcano rumbles, the arm bounces, and the pen moves up and down, **[4](G) leaving** marks on a piece of paper. The stronger the movement of the earth, the more the pen moves.

當地震發生，或火山發出隆隆聲時，臂狀物就會上下震動，使得墨水筆也隨之上下移動，並在一張紙上留下痕跡。地球震動的力量越大，筆移動的幅度也就越大。

volcano〔vɑl'keno〕*n.* 火山
rumble〔'rʌmbḷ〕*v.* 發出隆隆聲　　mark〔mɑrk〕*n.* 痕跡
「the + 比較級…the + 比較級」，表「愈…就愈～」。
movement〔'muvmənt〕*n.* 移動；震動

4. (**G**) 筆會上下移動，「留下」痕跡，選 (G) *leaving*。

When an earthquake [5](D) does occur, geologists measure the height of the pen marks to [6](F) figure out how strong it was. A number from one to nine is assigned to each quake, [7](C) depending on its strength: nine indicates the strongest quake, and one, the weakest. The scale is so designed that each number indicates a quake ten times [8](I) more powerful than the previous number.

當地震真的發生時，地質學家會測量筆跡的高度，以算出地震的強度。每一個地震可視其強度，分爲一到九級：九級是最強的地震，而一級則是最弱的。根據地震等級的設計，每一級地震的強度，比前一級要強十倍。

measure〔'mɛʒɚ〕*v.* 測量　　height〔haɪt〕*n.* 高度
assign〔ə'saɪn〕*v.* 分配；指定給
quake〔kwek〕*n.* 地震（= *earthquake*）
strength〔strɛŋθ〕*n.* 強度　　indicate〔'ɪndə,ket〕*v.* 表示
scale〔skel〕*n.* 等級　　design〔dɪ'zaɪn〕*v.* 設計
time〔taɪm〕*n.* 倍　　powerful〔'pauɚfəl〕*adj.* 強有力的
previous〔'priviəs〕*adj.* 之前的

5. (**D**) 加強動詞語氣，用 do, did, does 加原形動詞，表「眞的～」，依句意，選 (D) *does*。

6. (**F**) 測量筆跡的高度，來「算出」地震的強度，選 (F) *figure out*。

7. (**C**) depend on 表「視～而定」，在此應用分詞形式，故選 (C) *depending on*。

8. (**I**) 由空格後的 than 可知，此處爲比較級，故選 (I) *more*。

An earthquake that ⁹(H) measures seven or above is considered a major earthquake. The scale of numbers is called the Richter scale ¹⁰(A) after Charles Richter, the scientist who invented this method of measuring earthquakes.

七級以上的地震，被認爲是強烈地震。一至九級，被稱爲芮氏地震分等標準，它是以查爾斯芮克特的名字命名，查爾斯芮克特就是這種地震測量方法的發明人。

consider〔kən'sɪdɚ〕*v.* 認爲
major〔'medʒɚ〕*adj.* 重大的
the Richter scale 芮氏地震分等標準
scientist〔'saɪəntɪst〕*n.* 科學家
invent〔ɪn'vɛnt〕*v.* 發明
method〔'mɛθəd〕*n.* 方法

9. (**H**) *measure*〔'mɛʒɚ〕*v.* (測量後)有…(大、強度、長、寬、高)

10. (**A**) *be called after* 以～的名字命名 (= *be named after*)

TEST 19

說明： 第 1 至 10 題，每題一個空格。請依文意在文章後所提供的 (A) 到
(J) 選項中分別選出最適當者。

Taiwan has emerged ___1___ the world's second-most
populous country in terms of population density, behind only
Bangladesh, an official ___2___ the Ministry of the Interior (MOI)
said. As of June, Taiwan's population totaled 22,275,660, with
the density reaching 619 persons per square kilometer, said the
official, quoting MOI-compiled statistics. The official also cited
the 2001 World Population Data Sheet ___3___ the U.S. Population
Reference Bureau as showing that Bangladesh's population
density has reached 927.09 persons, ranking first ___4___
countries or areas with populations ___5___ more than 10 million.

According to the U.S. data, ___6___ Bangladesh are Taiwan,
South Korea, the Netherlands, Belgium, Japan, India, Sri Lanka,
the ___7___ and England. Mainland China was ranked 18th, with
a population density of 133.76 persons, but the total number of
its population has reached 1,280,600,000, the highest in the
world, ___8___ by India, the United States, Indonesia, ___9___,
Pakistan, the ___10___ Federation, Bangladesh, Japan and Nigeria.

(A) followed   (B) as   (C) Russian   (D) Brazil
(E) by   (F) among   (G) of   (H) following
(I) Philippines   (J) from

TEST 19 詳解

Taiwan has emerged [1](B) as the world's second-most populous country in terms of population density, behind only Bangladesh, an official [2](J) from the Ministry of the Interior (MOI) said. As of June, Taiwan's population totaled 22,275,660, with the density reaching 619 persons per square kilometer, said the official, quoting MOI-compiled statistics.

根據內政部一位官員指出，就人口密度而言，台灣已經成為全世界人口第二稠密的國家了，僅次於孟加拉。該官員引用內政部所編輯的統計數字指出，到六月為止，台灣的人口總數已達到 22,275,660 人，人口密度達到每平方公里 619 人。

emerge〔ɪ'mɝdʒ〕v. 出現
populous〔'pɑpjələs〕adj. 人口稠密的
in terms of~ 以~觀點來看　　population〔ˌpɑpjə'leʃən〕n. 人口
density〔'dɛnsətɪ〕n. 密度　　Bangladesh〔'bæŋglə'dɛʃ〕n. 孟加拉
official〔ə'fɪʃəl〕n. 官員　　ministry〔'mɪnɪstrɪ〕n. 部
interior〔ɪn'tɪrɪɚ〕n. 內政
the Ministry of the Interior 內政部
as of 到~為止　　total〔'totl〕v. 總數達到
square〔skwɛr〕adj. 平方的　　quote〔kwot〕v. 引用
compile〔kəm'paɪl〕v. 編輯
statistics〔stə'tɪstɪks〕n. pl. 統計數字

1.(**B**) 台灣已出現「成為」全世界第二，選 (B) *as*。

2.(**J**) 該官員「來自」內政部，選 (J) *from*。

The official also cited the 2001 World Population Data Sheet [3](E) by
the U.S. Population Reference Bureau as showing that Bangladesh's
population density has reached 927.09 persons, ranking first
[4](F) among countries or areas with populations [5](G) of more than 10
million.

該官員也引用美國人口資料局所做的,二〇〇一年世界人口資料表,表中
顯示,孟加拉的人口密度已達到 927.09 人,在人口總數超過一千萬的國家
或地區中,排名第一。

cite〔saɪt〕v. 引用　　***data sheet*** 資料表
reference〔'rɛfərəns〕n. 參考
bureau〔'bjʊro〕n. 局　　rank〔ræŋk〕v. 排名

3. (**E**) 根據句意,該資料表由美國做的,為被動用法,選 (E) ***by***。

4. (**F**) 表「在～當中」排名第一,選 (F) ***among***。

5. (**G**) 表示一個國家有多少人口,用 have a population ***of***～,
選 (G)。

According to the U.S. data, [6](H) following Bangladesh are
Taiwan, South Korea, the Netherlands, Belgium, Japan, India, Sri
Lanka, the [7](I) Philippines and England.

根據美國的資料,排在孟加拉後面的是:台灣、南韓、荷蘭、比利時、
日本、印度、斯里蘭卡、菲律賓和英國。

Korea〔ko'riə〕n. 韓國　　***South Korea*** 南韓
Netherlands〔'nɛðələndz〕n. 荷蘭 (= *Holland*)

Belgium (ˈbɛldʒɪəm) *n.* 比利時　　India (ˈɪndɪə) *n.* 印度
Sri Lanka (ˌsriˈlæŋkə) 斯里蘭卡

6. (**H**) 本句原爲 Taiwan, South Korea,…and England are
    following Bangladesh，在此將補語置於句首，主詞和 be
    動詞倒裝，故選 (H)。

7. (**I**) 國家名稱專有名詞若爲複數形，要加 the，由此可知此處應選
    (I) *Philippines*。　*the Philippines* 菲律賓

Mainland China was ranked 18th, with a population density of
133.76 persons, but the total number of its population has reached
1,280,600,000, the highest in the world, [8](A) followed by India,
the United States, Indonesia, [9](D) Brazil, Pakistan, the [10](C) Russian
Federation, Bangladesh, Japan and Nigeria.

中國大陸排名第十八，人口密度是每平方公里 133.76 人，但它的人口總數
已達到 1,280,600,000 人，爲全世界第一，接著是印度、美國、印尼、巴西、
巴基斯坦、俄羅斯共和國、孟加拉、日本和奈及利亞。

mainland (ˈmenˌlænd) *n.* 大陸　　*Mainland China* 中國大陸
Indonesia (ˌɪndoˈniʃə) *n.* 印尼
Pakistan (ˌpækɪˈstæn) *n.* 巴基斯坦
Nigeria (naɪˈdʒɪrɪə) *n.* 奈及利亞

8. (**A**) 由空格後的 by 可知，此處爲被動，故選 (A) *followed*。

9. (**D**) *Brazil* (brəˈzɪl) *n.* 巴西

10. (**C**) *Russian* (ˈrʌʃən) *adj.* 俄國的
    federation (ˌfɛdəˈreʃən) *n.* 聯邦
    the Russian Federation 俄羅斯共和國

TEST 20

說明： 第 1 至 10 題，每題一個空格。請依文意在文章後所提供的 (A) 到
(J) 選項中分別選出最適當者。

The Internet is the world's "___1___ of networks" linking
together millions of computer systems, ___2___, news services,
and libraries to create a ___3___ information resource.

Previously available to only selected universities, the door
is now open ___4___ individuals and companies. ___5___ each
new opportunity for positive development, there are also some
risks. ___6___ is one of them, especially in ___7___ to credit
card numbers and other personal financial information. All
users are advised to take the ___8___ to secure their information
in their company by using software that protects information
they send and receive over the Internet.

"Safenet" is available ___9___ cost to all the computer
users. Just send $15 to the following address: P.O. Box 17345
San Francisco, CA. Clear installation ___10___ can be obtained
through E-mail, Safenet@INT.com.

(A) at   (B) network   (C) instructions

(D) to   (E) unified   (F) with

(G) theft   (H) databases   (I) regard

(J) precaution

TEST 20 詳解

The Internet is the world's "[1](B) network of networks" linking together millions of computer systems, [2](H) databases, news services, and libraries to create a [3](E) unified information resource.

網際網路是電腦網路中的網路，把數百萬的電腦系統、資料庫、新聞資料服務站，以及圖書館連結在一起，創造出統一的資訊來源。

Internet ('ɪntə͵nɛt) *n.* 網際網路
link (lɪŋk) *v.* 連結　　system ('sɪstəm) *n.* 系統
create (krɪ'et) *v.* 創造
information (͵ɪnfə'meʃən) *n.* 資訊
resource (rɪ'sors) *n.* 資源；來源

1. (**B**) 網際網路是網路中的「網路」，選 (B) ***network*** ('nɛt͵wɜk) *n.* 電腦網路。

2. (**H**) 網際網路連結數百萬的電腦系統、「資料庫」、新聞資料服務站，以及圖書館，選 (H) ***databases*** ('detə͵besɪz) *n. pl.* 資料庫。

3. (**E**) 用來創造「統一的」資訊來源，選 (E) ***unified*** ('junə͵faɪd) *adj.* 統一的。

Previously available to only selected universities, the door is now open [4](D) to individuals and companies. [5](F) With each new opportunity for positive development, there are also some risks.

之前，網際網路只供特定的大學使用，現在則開放給個人及公司使用。隨著帶來正面發展的每一個新機會，網際網路也有一些風險。

previously〔'prɪvɪəslɪ〕*adv.* 之前
available〔ə'veləbḷ〕*adj.* 可供～使用的
selected〔sə'lɛktɪd〕*adj.* 特定的
individual〔͵ɪndə'vɪdʒʊəl〕*n.* 個人
company〔'kʌmpənɪ〕*n.* 公司
positive〔'pɑzətɪv〕*adj.* 正面的
development〔dɪ'vɛləpmənt〕*n.* 發展
risk〔rɪsk〕*n.* 風險

4.(**D**) *be open to* 可供～使用的（= *be available to*）

5.(**F**)「伴隨」網路發展，有一些風險，選 (F) *With*。

⁶(G) Theft is one of them, especially in ⁷(I) regard to credit card numbers and other personal financial information. All users are advised to take the ⁸(J) precaution to secure their information in their company by using software that protects information they send and receive over the Internet.

偷竊（資料）就是其中一個，特別是有關信用卡的卡號，及其他個人的財務資訊。所有使用者都被建議，要採取預防措施，藉由保護網際網路上傳送及接收資訊的軟體，來確保他們公司的資訊。

financial〔faɪ'nænʃəl〕*adj.* 財務的
advise〔əd'vaɪz〕*v.* 建議　　take〔tek〕*v.* 採取
secure〔sɪ'kjʊr〕*v.* 保護　　software〔'sɔft͵wɛr〕*n.* 軟體
send〔sɛnd〕*v.* 傳送　　receive〔rɪ'siv〕*v.* 接收

6. (**G**) 「偷竊」就是風險之一，選 (G) *theft*〔θɛft〕*n.* 偷竊。

7. (**I**) *in regard to* 關於（ = *about* = *regarding* ）

8. (**J**) 所有的使用者都被建議，要採取「預防措施」，選 (J)
   precaution〔prɪˋkɔʃən〕*n.* 預防措施。

"Safenet" is available [9](A) at cost to all the computer users.
Just send $15 to the following address: P.O. Box 17345 San
Francisco, CA. Clear installation [10](C) instructions can be obtained
through E-mail, Safenet@INT.com.

　　所有的電腦使用者，都可以用成本價買到「安全網路」軟體。只要寄
15 元到以下的地址：加州，舊金山郵政 17345 號信箱。透過 Safenet@
@INT.com. 此網址，可取得清楚的安裝說明。

available〔əˋveləbḷ〕*adj.* 買得到的
cost〔kɔst〕*n.* 成本　　address〔əˋdrɛs; ˋædrɛs〕*n.* 網址
P.O. Box 郵政信箱（ = *Post Office Box* ）
San Francisco〔ˌsænfrənˋsɪsko〕*n.* 舊金山
CA 加州（ = *California* ）
clear〔klɪr〕*adj.* 清楚的
installation〔ˌɪnstəˋleʃən〕*n.* 安裝
obtain〔əbˋten〕*v.* 獲得

9. (**A**) *at cost* 以成本價

10. (**C**) 可以經由網路，取得清楚的安裝「說明」，選 (C) *instructions*
    〔ɪnˋstrʌkʃənz〕*n. pl.* 說明。

TEST 21

說明： 第 1 至 10 題，每題一個空格。請依文意在文章後所提供的 (A) 到
(J) 選項中分別選出最適當者。

Electronic Cupid Signals the Way to Love

There is a certain romantic buzz around popular teenage
___1___ in Tokyo — and the sound is coming from a pocket-size
transmitter, called the Love Connection, that helps youngsters
meet up with their peers. If you want to get ___2___, first select the
gender of the person you wish to meet, and then pick out a choice
of three date patterns: "just to talk," "let's go to karaoke," or "let's
kiss." The transmitter will then identify anyone nearby who is on
the same ___3___ as you — simply ___4___ the beeping noise to meet
your electronic soul mate. The gadget is one of several innovative
date-___5___ trends in Tokyo. Another method is through pager
___6___, in which teens ___7___ to personal ads in magazines placed
by those seeking "Beeping Friends." But 19-year-old Carol, who
has tried these fads, is ___8___. "There are a lot of geeks out there
trying to find dates through technology," she says. "But the good
ones need no help. The old-___9___ pick-up is still the most exciting
way to meet someone." East or West, eye ___10___ is the best.

(A) messages (B) contact (C) follow   (D) hangouts
(E) connected (F) finding (G) wavelength (H) unimpressed
(I) respond   (J) fashioned

TEST 21 詳解

Electronic Cupid Signals the Way to Love

There is a certain romantic buzz around popular teenage ¹**(D) hangouts** in Tokyo — and the sound is coming from a pocket-size transmitter, called the Love Connection, that helps youngsters meet up with their peers.

電子丘比特告訴你愛在何方

在東京,現在有某個浪漫的嗶嗶聲,出現在很受歡迎的青少年常去之處——這個聲音來自一個叫「愛的連接」的小型發報器,可以幫助青少年遇見他們的同儕。

electronic〔ɪ͵lɛkˈtrɑnɪk〕*adj.* 電子的
Cupid〔ˈkjupɪd〕*n.*(愛神)丘比特　　signal〔ˈsɪgnl〕*v.* 發出信號
buzz〔bʌz〕*n.* 嗶嗶聲　　pocket-size〔ˈpɑkɪt͵saɪz〕*adj.* 小型的
transmitter〔trænsˈmɪtɚ〕*n.* 發報器
connection〔kəˈnɛkʃən〕*n.* 連接　　youngster〔ˈjʌŋstɚ〕*n.* 青少年
meet up with 遇到　　peer〔pɪr〕*n.* 同儕

1.(**D**)***hangout***〔ˈhæŋ͵aʊt〕*n.* 常去之處

If you want to get ²**(E) connected**, first select the gender of the person you wish to meet, and then pick out a choice of three date patterns: "just to talk," "let's go to karaoke," or "let's kiss." The transmitter will then identify anyone nearby who is on the same ³**(G) wavelength** as you — simply ⁴**(C) follow** the beeping noise to meet your electronic soul mate.

如果你也想連接上,首先挑選你想遇見的人的性別,然後挑選三種約會模式其中之一:「只是談話」、「我們去唱卡拉 OK」、「我們親吻吧」。這個發報器接著就會辨識,附近有誰和你的波長一樣——你只要跟著嗶嗶聲走,就可以遇見你的電子情人。

    select〔sə'lɛkt〕v. 選擇
    gender〔'dʒɛndɚ〕n. 性別　　***pick out*** 挑選出
    pattern〔'pætɚn〕n. 模式
    identify〔aɪ'dɛntə,faɪ〕v. 辨認　　beep〔bip〕v. 發出嗶嗶聲
    noise〔nɔɪz〕n. 聲音　　***soul mate*** 情人

2. (**E**) ***connect***〔kə'nɛkt〕v. 連接

3. (**G**) ***wavelength***〔'wev,lɛŋθ〕n. 波長

4. (**C**) 「跟著」嗶嗶聲走,選 (C) ***follow*** 。

The gadget is one of several innovative date-[5](F) finding trends in Tokyo. Another method is through pager [6](A) messages, in which teens [7](I) respond to personal ads in magazines placed by those seeking "Beeping Friends."

這個裝置在東京,是數種尋找約會對象的創新趨勢之一。另一個方法則是透過呼叫器留言,回覆私人廣告,這些廣告是那些想利用呼叫器找朋友的人,在雜誌上刊登的。

    gadget〔'gædʒɪt〕n. 裝置
    innovative〔'ɪnə,vetɪv〕adj. 創新的
    date〔det〕n. 約會對象　　trend〔trɛnd〕n. 趨勢
    pager〔'pedʒɚ〕n. 呼叫器 (= *beeper*)　　seek〔sik〕v. 尋找

5. (**F**) 依句意，這是「尋找」約會對象的**趨勢**，find 在此為主動，用現在分詞 date-***finding*** trends，選 (F)。

6. (**A**) ***message*** ('mɛsɪdʒ) *n.* 留言

7. (**I**) ***respond*** (rɪ'spɑnd) *v.* 回應；回覆 < *to* >

But 19-year-old Carol, who has tried these fads, is [8](H) unimpressed. "There are a lot of geeks out there trying to find dates through technology," she says. "But the good ones need no help. The old-[9](J) fashioned pick-up is still the most exciting way to meet someone." East or West, eye [10](B) contact is the best.

但是，已嘗試過這些流行玩意、十九歲的卡蘿，卻不以為然。她說：「外面有很多變態，想透過科技來尋找約會對象。但好的對象是不需要幫助的。傳統的方法仍然是認識別人最刺激的方法。」不論東方西方，目光接觸最棒。

> fad (fæd) *n.* 流行
> geek (gik) *n.* 怪胎；變態　　***out there*** 在那邊
> technology (tɛk'nɑlədʒɪ) *n.* 科技
> pick-up ('pɪkˏʌp) *n.* 認識人的方法

8. (**H**) ***unimpressed*** (ˏʌnɪm'prɛst) *adj.* 沒有好印象的

9. (**J**) old-***fashioned*** ('old'fæʃənd) *adj.* 不流行的；傳統的

10. (**B**) ***contact*** ('kɑntækt) *n.* 接觸
　　　eye contact 目光接觸

TEST 22

說明： 第 1 至 10 題，每題一個空格。請依文意在文章後所提供的 (A) 到
(J) 選項中分別選出最適當者。

A __1__ of tourists visiting the U.S. face more than the
language __2__ when they visit New York or other large
American cities. How to tip is quite a problem to them.

France, __3__ many other European countries, has a "tip-
included" policy, which means the service is included in the
__4__. But if a customer is especially satisfied with the
service, he or she might leave an extra dollar or two on the
table. A __5__ official told the story of a French visitor who
felt insulted when an American __6__ followed him to the
door, __7__ him the dollar he had left on the table as a tip
and told him, "I think you need this dollar __8__ I do. Take it."
The French visitor __9__ that the tip had already been included.

Just how much should a person tip? "In America, 15% is
acceptable and 20% is preferable," said John Tuchiano, the
spokesman for the hotel and restaurant employees __10__.

(A) assumed   (B) number   (C) union   (D) bill
(E) as well as (F) waiter   (G) tourism   (H) barrier
(I) handed   (J) more than

TEST 22 詳解

A ¹(B) number of tourists visiting the U.S. face more than the
language ²(H) barrier when they visit New York or other large
American cities. How to tip is quite a problem to them.

很多去美國旅行的旅客，在造訪紐約或其他美國的大都市時，所面臨
的不只是語言障礙。如何付小費對他們而言，就是一個相當頭痛的問題。

tourist (ˋturɪst) *n.* 旅客　　face (fes) *v.* 面臨
more than 不只　　tip (tɪp) *v.* 付小費

1. (**B**) ***a number of*** 很多

2. (**H**) ***language barrier*** 語言障礙

France, ³(E) as well as many other European countries, has a
"tip-included" policy, which means the service is included in the
⁴(D) bill. But if a customer is especially satisfied with the service,
he or she might leave an extra dollar or two on the table. A
⁵(G) tourism official told the story of a French visitor who felt
insulted when an American ⁶(F) waiter followed him to the door,
⁷(I) handed him the dollar he had left on the table as a tip and told
him, "I think you need this dollar ⁸(J) more than I do. Take it." The
French visitor ⁹(A) assumed that the tip had already been included.

法國以及許多其他的歐洲國家，都是「小費內含」的政策，意思是服
務費已包含在帳單裡面。但是如果顧客對於服務特別滿意，他（她）可以
在桌上多留個一兩塊錢。一位旅遊業的官員說了一個法國旅客的故事，他
走到餐廳門口時，一位美國服務生跟著他，並將他留在桌上的小費交還給
他，服務生說：「我想你會比我更需要這筆錢。拿去吧。」法國旅客覺得
倍受污辱。他以為小費已經包含在帳單裡面了。

include〔ɪn'klud〕*v.* 包括　　policy〔'pɑləsɪ〕*n.* 政策

customer〔'kʌstəmə〕*n.* 顧客　　*be satisfied with* 對～很滿意

leave〔liv〕*v.* 留下　　extra〔'ɛkstrə〕*adj.* 額外的

official〔ə'fɪʃəl〕*n.* 官員　　insulted〔ɪn'sʌltɪd〕*adj.* (受到)污辱的

3. (**E**) 法國「以及」許多其他的歐洲國家，都是「小費內含」的政策，
選 (E) *as well as*。

4. (**D**) 「小費內含」的政策意思是服務費包含在「帳單」裡面，故選
(D) *bill*〔bɪl〕*n.* 帳單。

5. (**G**) 一位「旅遊業」官員說了一個法國旅客的故事，選 (G) *tourism*
〔'tʊrɪzəm〕*n.* 觀光業；旅遊業。

6. (**F**) 一位美國「服務生」跟著他到門口，交還小費，選 (F) *waiter*。

7. (**I**) 「交給」他小費，選動詞 (I) *hand*〔hænd〕*v.* 交給。

8. (**J**) 我想你會「比」我「更」需要這筆錢，選 (J) *more than*。

9. (**A**) 法國旅客「以為」小費已經包含在內，選 (A) *assume*
〔ə'sjum〕*v.* 認為。

Just how much should a person tip? "In America, 15% is
acceptable and 20% is preferable," said John Tuchiano, the
spokesman for the hotel and restaurant employees [10](C) union.

我們到底要付多少小費？飯店及餐廳員工工會的發言人，約翰杜奇安
諾說：「在美國，帳單的百分之十五尚可接受，百分之二十則更好」。

acceptable〔ək'sɛptəbl̩〕*adj.* 可以接受的

preferable〔'prɛfərəbl̩〕*adj.* 更好的

spokesman〔'spoksmən〕*n.* 發言人　　employee〔ˌɛmplɔɪ'i〕*n.* 員工

10. (**C**) 飯店及餐廳員工「工會」，選 (C) *union*〔'junjən〕*n.* 工會。

TEST 23

說明： 第 1 至 10 題，每題一個空格。請依文意在文章後所提供的 (A) 到 (J) 選項中分別選出最適當者。

Andorra is a small mountainous country in southwestern Europe. It is bordered on the north and east by France, and on the south and west by Spain. The capital is Andorra la Vella with a ___1___ of approximately 25,000. The official language is Catalan, but French and Spanish are widely spoken.

The tourist who likes to get off the ___2___ track will appreciate the peace and quiet of Andorra, one of the few ___3___ countries without an airport. Whether you want to relax after a hike in a natural spa, or visit some of the finest galleries of plastic arts in Europe, Andorra has ___4___ for you. If you would like a little more excitement, Andorra's world-renowned music festivals may be ___5___ what you need. For Jazz fans, there is the international jazz festival in July; for classical music buffs the Ordino Festival takes place in September; and ___6___ the summer, you can see and hear folk song and dance in Andorra la Vella.

You must not leave Andorra ___7___ visiting Europe's finest ___8___ shopping centers. Andorra has long been a tax haven, and this fact is ___9___ in the range and quality of items as well ___10___ some of the most reasonable prices in Europe.

(A) duty-free   (B) population   (C) as
(D) reflected   (E) remaining   (F) something
(G) just   (H) throughout   (I) without
(J) beaten

TEST 23 詳解

Andorra is a small mountainous country in southwestern Europe. It is bordered on the north and east by France, and on the south and west by Spain. The capital is Andorra la Vella with a ¹(B) population of approximately 25,000. The official language is Catalan, but French and Spanish are widely spoken.

安道爾共和國位於西南歐，是一個面積不大的山區國家。它的北部和東部毗鄰法國，南部和西部則連接西班牙。安道爾共和國的首都是 Andorra la Vella，人口大約有兩萬五千人。官方語言是加泰隆尼亞語，但是法語和西班牙語也被廣泛使用。

Andorra (æn'dɔrə) *n.* 安道爾共和國
  (位於法國和西班牙交界之東庇里牛斯山中)
mountainous ('mauntnəs) *adj.* 山地的
border ('bɔrdə) *v.* 鄰接   France (fræns) *n.* 法國
Spain (spen) *n.* 西班牙   capital ('kæpətḷ) *n.* 首都
approximately (ə'prɑksəmɪtlɪ) *adv.* 大約
official (ə'fɪʃəl) *adj.* 官方的   Catalan ('kætḷən) *n.* 加泰隆尼亞語
French (frɛntʃ) *n.* 法語   Spanish ('spænɪʃ) *n.* 西班牙語
widely ('waɪdlɪ) *adv.* 廣泛地

1. (**B**) 由後面的 of approximately 25,000 可知，此處是指「人口」，故選 (B) *population* (ˌpɑpjə'leʃən) *n.* 人口。

The tourist who likes to get off the ²(J) beaten track will appreciate the peace and quiet of Andorra, one of the few ³(E) remaining countries without an airport. Whether you want to relax after a hike in a natural spa, or visit some of the finest galleries of

plastic arts in Europe, Andorra has [4](F) something for you. If you
would like a little more excitement, Andorra's world-renowned
music festivals may be [5](G) just what you need. For Jazz fans, there
is the international jazz festival in July; for classical music buffs
the Ordino Festival takes place in September; and [6](H) throughout
the summer, you can see and hear folk song and dance in Andorra
la Vella.

　　討厭和其他觀光客人擠人的旅客，一定會喜歡安道爾共和國的安寧與
靜謐，它是少數幾個還沒有機場的國家。不論你想在健行後，到溫泉放鬆
一下，還是想參觀全歐洲最好的幾家塑膠藝品美術館，安道爾共和國都
有。如果你想要多一點刺激的玩意兒，世界聞名的安道爾音樂節，正是你
所需要的。七月份的國際爵士節，可以滿足所有爵士迷；對古典樂迷來說，
九月舉行的 Ordino 節，絕不會讓他們敗興而歸；而且，整個暑假期間，
你可以在首都 Andorra la Vella 欣賞到民俗歌舞表演。

　　appreciate〔ə'priʃɪ‚et〕v. 欣賞　　peace〔pis〕n. 安寧；安靜
　　quiet〔'kwaɪət〕n. 寧靜　　hike〔haɪk〕n. 健行
　　spa〔spɑ〕n. 溫泉　　gallery〔'gælərɪ〕n. 畫廊；美術館
　　plastic〔'plæstɪk〕adj. 塑膠的
　　excitement〔ɪk'saɪtmənt〕n. 興奮；刺激的事物
　　renowned〔rɪ'naʊnd〕adj. 有名的
　　festival〔'fɛstəvl̩〕n. 節日；慶典
　　fan〔fæn〕n. 迷　　jazz〔dʒæz〕n. 爵士樂
　　buff〔bʌf〕n. 迷（=*fan*）　　*take place* 舉行
　　folk〔fok〕adj. 民謠的

2.(**J**) *off the beaten track*　（地點）人跡罕至的；鮮為人知的

3.(**E**) 安道爾為「僅存的」少數幾個沒有機場的國家，故選 (E)
　　remaining〔rɪ'menɪŋ〕adj. 剩下的。

4. (**F**) 這裡需要名詞做 have 的受詞，依句意，安道爾有他們想要的
「東西」，故選 (F) *something*。

5. (**G**) 「正」是你需要的，用 *just* 來加強語氣，故選 (G)。

6. (**H**) *throughout*〔θruˋaʊt〕*prep.* 整個；在～期間。

You must not leave Andorra [7](I) without visiting Europe's finest
[8](A) duty-free shopping centers. Andorra has long been a tax haven,
and this fact is [9](D) reflected in the range and quality of items as well
[10](C) as some of the most reasonable prices in Europe.

　　來到安道爾共和國，絕對不能錯過歐洲最棒的免稅購物中心。安道爾
共和國一直以來，就是個免稅天堂，而這完全可以反應在商品的種類、品
質，以及踏遍歐洲也找不到的合理價格上。

> *shopping center* 購物中心　　tax〔tæks〕*n.* 稅金
> haven〔ˋhevən〕*n.* 避難所
> *tax haven* 稅率很低或免稅的地區（比喻為免稅天堂）
> range〔rendʒ〕*n.* 範圍　　quality〔ˋkwɑlətɪ〕*n.* 品質
> item〔ˋaɪtəm〕*n.* 東西　　reasonable〔ˋriznəbl〕*adj.* 合理的

7. (**I**) *not～without*… 為「雙重否定」的句型，表「每…必；無…
不」。

8. (**A**) 由後面的 a tax haven 可知，安道爾以「免稅天堂」著稱，故
應擁有「免稅」購物中心，故選 (A) *duty-free*〔ˋdjutɪˋfri〕*adj.*
免稅的。

9. (**D**) 安道爾為免稅天堂這件事，可以「反映」在商品的種類、品質，
及合理價格上，故選 (D) *reflected*〔rɪˋflɛktɪd〕*v.* 反映。

10. (**C**) *as well as* 以及

TEST 24

說明： 第 1 至 10 題，每題一個空格。請依文意在文章後所提供的 (A) 到
(J) 選項中分別選出最適當者。

All living things die eventually. In ecological ____1____,
the chemicals of living things are borrowed from the Earth,
and ____2____ death they return. All the material that every
animal, from the smallest fly to the largest elephant, takes
____3____ as food also returns to the Earth, as waste matter.
The dead material and waste matter ____4____ the diet of a
group of living ____5____ called decomposers. They include
a range of bacteria, fungi, and small animals that ____6____
down nature's wastes into even smaller pieces until all the
chemicals are released into the air, the soil, and the water,
making them ____7____ to other living things. Without the
carbon dioxide released during the process, all plant life
would die out. Without the oxygen that plants give out and
without the food that they supply, life would ____8____ to a
halt and all animals would ____9____. The decomposers are a
____10____ link in the natural cycle of life and death.

【建國中學期末考】

(A) break   (B) in   (C) grind   (D) vital
(E) terms   (F) starve   (G) at   (H) form
(I) available   (J) organisms

TEST 24 詳解

All living things die eventually. In ecological **¹(E) terms**, the chemicals of living things are borrowed from the Earth, and **²(G) at** death they return.

所有的生物最後都會死。照生態學上的說法,生物身上的化學物質是向地球借來的,所以死的時候就會歸還那些東西。

living〔'lɪvɪŋ〕*adj.* 活的　　***living things*** 生物
eventually〔ɪ'vɛntʃʊəlɪ〕*adv.* 最後
ecological〔ˌikə'lɑdʒɪkḷ〕*adj.* 生態學上的
chemical〔'kɛmɪkḷ〕*n.* 化學物質　　borrow〔'baro〕*v.* 借 (入)
Earth〔ɝθ〕*n.* 地球　　return〔rɪ'tɝn〕*v.* 歸還

1. **(E)** 依句意,照生態學上的「說法」,選 (E) ***terms***〔tɝmz〕*n. pl.* 說法。

2. **(G)** ***at death*** 死的時候

All the material that every animal, from the smallest fly to the largest elephant, takes **³(B) in** as food also returns to the Earth, as waste matter. The dead material and waste matter **⁴(H) form** the diet of a group of living **⁵(J) organisms** called decomposers.

從最小的蒼蠅到最大的大象,所有被動物當成食物吃掉的東西,都會以排泄物的形式,歸還給地球。死掉的東西和排泄物,會成爲一群生物的食物,這群生物叫作分解者。

material〔məˈtɪrɪəl〕*n.* 物質
fly〔flaɪ〕*n.* 蒼蠅　　elephant〔ˈɛləfənt〕*n.* 大象
waste〔west〕*adj.* 廢棄的　*n.* 廢棄物　　matter〔ˈmætɚ〕*n.* 物質
waste matter　（動物的）排泄物
diet〔ˈdaɪət〕*n.* 食物　　group〔grup〕*n.* 群
decomposer〔ˌdikəmˈpozɚ〕*n.* 分解者

3. (**B**) ***take in*** 吃掉

4. (**H**) 依句意，死掉的東西和排泄物會「成爲」一群生物的食物，
選 (H)***form***〔fɔrm〕*v.* 形成。

5. (**J**) 依句意，這群「生物」叫作分解者，選 (J) ***organisms***。
organism〔ˈɔrgənˌɪzəm〕*n.* 生物

They include a range of bacteria, fungi, and small animals that [6](A)
break down nature's wastes into even smaller pieces until all the
chemicals are released into the air, the soil, and the water, making
them [7](I) available to other living things.

它們的種類包括細菌、黴菌，和小動物，它們會把自然界的廢棄物，分解
成更小的碎片，直到所有化學物質都被釋放到空氣、土壤和水中，使其他
生物得以利用這些物質。

include〔ɪnˈklud〕*v.* 包括　　range〔rendʒ〕*n.* 範圍；類別
bacteria〔bækˈtɪrɪə〕*n. pl.* 細菌
fungi〔ˈfʌndʒaɪ〕*n. pl.* 黴菌（單數爲 fungus〔ˈfʌŋgəs〕）
nature〔ˈnetʃɚ〕*n.* 大自然　　even〔ˈivən〕*adv.* 更加
piece〔pis〕*n.* 碎片　　release〔rɪˈlis〕*v.* 釋放
soil〔sɔɪl〕*n.* 土壤

6. (**A**) *break down* 分解

7. (**I**) 依句意，使其他生物「得以利用」這些物質，選 (I) *available*
〔 əˈvɛləbḷ 〕 *adj.* 可利用的；可獲得的。

Without the carbon dioxide released during the process, all plant
life would die out. Without the oxygen that plants give out and
without the food that they supply, life would **⁸(C) grind** to a halt
and all animals would **⁹(F) starve**. The decomposers are a **¹⁰(D) vital**
link in the natural cycle of life and death.

如果沒有經由這個過程所釋放出的二氧化碳，所有的植物都會枯死。如果
沒有植物所散發出來的氧氣，還有它們所提供的食物，生命就會慢慢停
止，而且所有的動物都會餓死。分解者在生與死的自然循環中，是非常重
要的一環。

> carbon〔ˈkɑrbən〕*n.* 碳
> dioxide〔darˈɑksaɪd〕*n.* 二氧化物　　*carbon dioxide* 二氧化碳
> process〔ˈprɑsɛs〕*n.* 過程　　life〔laɪf〕*n.* 生物
> *plant life* 植物　　*die out* 滅絕
> oxygen〔ˈɑksədʒən〕*n.* 氧　　*give out* 散發
> supply〔səˈplaɪ〕*v.* 提供　　halt〔hɔlt〕*n.* 停止
> link〔lɪŋk〕*n.* 環；節　　natural〔ˈnætʃərəl〕*adj.* 自然的
> cycle〔ˈsaɪkḷ〕*n.* 循環

8. (**C**) 依句意，生命就會「慢慢停止」，選 (C) *grind*〔graɪnd〕*v.* 磨碎。
grind to a halt 慢慢停止

9. (**F**) 依句意，而且所有的動物都會「餓死」，選 (F) *starve*〔stɑrv〕*v.*
餓死。

10. (**D**) 依句意，分解者在生與死的自然循環中，是「非常重要的」一環，
選 (D) *vital*〔ˈvaɪtḷ〕*adj.* 非常重要的。

TEST 25

說明： 第 1 至 10 題，每題一個空格。請依文意在文章後所提供的 (A) 到
(J) 選項中分別選出最適當者。

　　Antarctica is by measure the coldest, most remote and
most inhospitable of all the continents on the planet. Given
these frightening obstacles, it is ___1___ that it was the last of
the continents to be discovered, ___2___ masked behind barriers
of ice and dangerous seas. Its coast was first sighted in the early
19th century. Its interior was not to be probed ___3___ nearly a
century later, when expeditions ___4___ Scott and Amundsen
braved unimaginable hardship to ___5___ the South Pole in 1911.

　　Covering an area of 5.5 million square miles, and larger
than ___6___ Europe or Australia, Antarctica is only slightly
more ___7___ to us now than when it was first discovered. Of
the world's great land masses, it is the only one without a
___8___ human population. And there is good reason for it.
While Antarctica ___9___ have climate zones, these zones all
have one dominant feature ___10___ —— they are all very cold
indeed and thus deter people from living there. 【北模】

　　(A) led by 　　　　(B) permanent 　　　(C) does

　　(D) little wonder 　(E) either 　　　　(F) reach

　　(G) accessible 　　 (H) remaining 　　　(I) in common

　　(J) until

TEST 25 詳解

Antarctica is by measure the coldest, most remote and most inhospitable of all the continents on the planet.

根據測量，在地球上的所有大陸中，南極洲是最冷、最偏僻，而且最不適合居住的地方。

> Antarctica〔ænt'ɑrktɪkə〕*n.* 南極洲
> measure〔'mɛʒɚ〕*n.* 測量　　***by measure*** 根據測量
> remote〔rɪ'mot〕*adj.* 遙遠的；偏僻的
> inhospitable〔ɪn'hɑspɪtəbl̩〕*adj.* 不適合居住的
> continent〔'kɑntənənt〕*n.* 洲；大陸
> planet〔'plænɪt〕*n.* 行星；地球

Given these frightening obstacles, it is ¹(D) little wonder that it was the last of the continents to be discovered, ²(H) remaining masked behind barriers of ice and dangerous seas.

考慮到這些可怕的阻礙，也就難怪它是最後一塊被發現的大陸，它到現在仍然隱藏在一些阻礙背後，那就是冰塊與危險的海洋。

> given〔'gɪvən〕*prep.* 考慮到
> frightening〔'fraɪtənɪŋ〕*adj.* 令人害怕的；恐怖的
> obstacle〔'ɑbstəkl̩〕*n.* 阻礙
> last〔læst〕*n.* 最後的人（或事物）
> discover〔dɪ'skʌvɚ〕*v.* 發現
> mask〔mæsk〕*v.* 隱藏　　behind〔bɪ'haɪnd〕*adv.* 在後面
> barrier〔'bærɪɚ〕*n.* 阻礙

1. (**D**) *little wonder* 難怪 (= *no wonder*)。

2. (**H**) 依句意，它到現在「仍然」隱藏在一些阻礙背後，選 (H)
   remaining。　　*remain* ﹝rɪ'men﹞v. 仍然；依舊

Its coast was first sighted in the early 19ᵗʰ century. Its interior was

not to be probed ³(**J**) until nearly a century later, when expeditions

⁴(**A**) led by Scott and Amundsen braved unimaginable hardship to

⁵(**F**) reach the South Pole in 1911.

十九世紀初，人們第一次發現它的海岸。直到將近一個世紀之後，人們
才開始探索它的內部，在一九九一年，由史考特和阿孟森所率領的探險
隊，在勇敢地面對無法想像的艱難之後，才到達南極。

> coast ﹝kost﹞n. 海岸　　sight ﹝saɪt﹞v. 看出；發現
> century ﹝'sɛntʃərɪ﹞n. 世紀
> interior ﹝ɪn'tɪrɪɚ﹞n. 內部；內陸
> probe ﹝prob﹞v. 探索；探查　　nearly ﹝'nɪrlɪ﹞adv. 將近
> expedition ﹝‚ɛkspɪ'dɪʃən﹞n. 探險隊
> brave ﹝brev﹞v. 勇敢地面對；冒⋯之險
> unimaginable ﹝‚ʌnɪ'mædʒɪnəbḷ﹞adj. 無法想像的
> hardship ﹝'hardʃɪp﹞n. 艱難
> pole ﹝pol﹞n. 極；極地　　*the South Pole* 南極

3. (**J**) 根據句意，「直到」將近一個世紀之後，人們才開始探索它
   的內部，選 (J) *until*。

4. (**A**) 依句意，「由」史考特和阿孟森所「率領」的探險隊，選 (A)
   led by。　　*lead* ﹝lid﹞v. 率領 (三態變化為：lead-led-led)

5. (**F**) *reach* 〔 ritʃ 〕 *v.* 到達

Covering an area of 5.5 million square miles, and larger than
⁶**(E) either** Europe or Australia, Antarctica is only slightly more
⁷**(G) accessible** to us now than when it was first discovered.

　　南極洲的面積約有五百五十萬平方英哩，它比歐洲或澳洲還大，但是對我們來說，跟它最初被發現時比起來，它現在只有稍微比較容易到達。

cover〔ˈkʌvɚ〕 *v.* 佔；涵蓋　　area〔ˈɛrɪə〕 *n.* 面積
million〔ˈmɪljən〕 *adj.* 百萬的
square〔skwɛr〕 *adj.* 平方的　　mile〔maɪl〕 *n.* 英哩
Europe〔ˈjurəp〕 *n.* 歐洲
Australia〔ɔˈstreljə〕 *n.* 澳洲　　slightly〔ˈslaɪtlɪ〕 *adv.* 稍微

6. (**E**) 依句意，它比歐洲「或」澳洲還大，選 (E) *either*。

either A *or* B　A 或 B

比較：

　① neither A nor B　既不是 A，也不是 B
　② both A and B　A 和 B
　③ not A but B　不是 A，而是 B
　④ A as well as B　A 以及 B

7. (**G**) 依句意，它現在只有稍微比較「容易到達」，選 (G)

accessible〔 ækˈsɛsəbl̩ 〕 *adj.* 容易到達的。

Of the world's great land masses, it is the only one without a
⁸**(B) permanent** human population. And there is good reason for it.

在全世界的大陸中，南極洲是唯一沒有人群永久居住的地方。這件事是有正當理由的。

> mass〔mæs〕*n.* 團；塊　　***land mass*** 大陸
> population〔‚papjə'leʃən〕*n.* 族群　　reason〔'rizn̩〕*n.* 理由
> ***good reason*** 正當的理由

8. (**B**) 南極洲是唯一沒有人群「永久」居住的地方，選 (B)
permanent〔'pɝmənənt〕*adj.* 永久的。

While Antarctica [9](C) does have climate zones, these zones all have one dominant feature [10](I) in common——they are all very cold indeed and thus deter people from living there.

儘管南極洲的確有分氣候區，但是這些氣候區都有一個共同的主要特色——它們全都真的非常冷，所以打消了人們居住在那裡的念頭。

> while〔hwaɪl〕*conj.* 儘管
> climate〔'klaɪmɪt〕*n.* 氣候　　zone〔zon〕*n.* 區域
> dominant〔'damənənt〕*adj.* 主要的
> feature〔'fitʃɚ〕*n.* 特色
> indeed〔ɪn'did〕*adv.* 真地；的確　　thus〔ðʌs〕*adv.* 因此
> deter〔dɪ'tɝ〕*v.* 使…打消念頭；妨礙；阻止 <*from* >

9. (**C**) do, did, does 接原形動詞，表「真的~；的確~」，依句
意選 (C) ***does***。

10. (**I**) 但是這些氣候區都有一個「共同的」主要特色，選 (I)
in common 共同的。
common〔'kamən〕*adj.* 共同的

TEST 26

The Chinese Horoscope, which plays an important part in the daily lives of many Asians, was developed around 12 animal signs. The names of the signs come from a Buddhist myth. Before Buddha left the earth, he called all the animals to come, only 12 of ___1___ appeared. The rat was the first, followed by the ox, tiger, rabbit ___2___. To reward the animals, Buddha named each year after them in the order of their arrival. For Chinese people, the animal ruling the year when one was born is ___3___ to have a great influence on his fate. To have good luck, people look to the Horoscope when ___4___ with important events, ___5___ choosing husbands or wives. Take a Goat woman for example. The Snake man is said to make the best spouse for her,

___6___ marrying a Dog man might lead to an unhappy

marriage. In addition, one has the ___7___ of the animal

ruling his birth. A person born in the year of the Rabbit,

for instance, should be "sweet and gentle but timid." It

seems that certain Chinese signs have bad and nasty

___8___ in Western culture. For Westerners, a rat is

someone who ___9___ others out of their money and a

pig is a dirty and greedy person. However, both animals

are ___10___: the Rat for its creativity and the Pig for

its intelligence. 【中山女中期中考】

(A) dealing　　(B) characteristics　　(C) respected

(D) such as　　(E) which　　(F) supposed

(G) tricks　　(H) while　　(I) images

(J) and so on

TEST 26 詳解

The Chinese Horoscope, which plays an important part in the daily lives of many Asians, was developed around 12 animal signs. The names of the signs come from a Buddhist myth.

在許多亞洲人的日常生活中，十二生肖扮演著很重要的角色，它是以十二種生肖爲基礎，所發展出來的。這些生肖的名稱，是來自佛教的神話故事。

horoscope〔'hɔrə,skop〕*n.* 占星術；黃道十二宮
Chinese Horoscope 十二生肖　　play〔ple〕*v.* 扮演
part〔part〕*n.* 角色　　daily〔'delɪ〕*adj.* 日常的
Asian〔'eʃən〕*n.* 亞洲人　　develop〔dɪ'vɛləp〕*v.* 發展
around〔ə'raund〕*prep.* 以…爲基礎
sign〔saɪn〕*n.*【天文】宮；星座；生肖　　***animal sign*** 生肖
Buddhist〔'budɪst〕*adj.* 佛教的　　myth〔mɪθ〕*n.* 神話故事

Before Buddha left the earth, he called all the animals to come, only 12 of **[1](E) which** appeared. The rat was the first, followed by the ox, tiger, rabbit **[2](J) and so on**. To reward the animals, Buddha named each year after them in the order of their arrival.

在佛陀升天之前，祂把所有的動物召喚過來，但只有十二種動物來。老鼠是第一個到的，接著是牛、老虎、兔子等。爲了獎勵這些動物，佛陀就依到達的順序，用牠們的名字，來替每一年命名。

Buddha〔'budə〕*n.* 佛陀 (釋迦牟尼的尊稱)
earth〔ɝθ〕*n.* 塵世；人間　　call〔kɔl〕*v.* 召喚
appear〔ə'pɪr〕*v.* 出現；來到　　rat〔ræt〕*n.* 老鼠

follow〔'falo〕v. 跟隨　　***followed by***… 接著就是…

ox〔aks〕n. 牛　　reward〔rɪ'wɔrd〕v. 獎賞；答謝

name〔nem〕v. 命名　　***name A after B*** 以 A 的名字幫 B 命名

order〔'ɔrdɚ〕n. 順序　　arrival〔ə'raɪvl〕n. 到達

1. (**E**) 空格應填具有連接詞作用，又可代替先行詞 the animals 的關係代名詞，故選 (E) ***which***。

2. (**J**) 依句意，接著是牛、老虎、兔子「等」，選 (J) ***and so on***「等等」(= *and so forth*)。

For Chinese people, the animal ruling the year when one was born is [3]**(F) supposed** to have a great influence on his fate. To have good luck, people look to the Horoscope when [4]**(A) dealing** with important events, [5]**(D) such as** choosing husbands or wives.

對中國人來說，當一個人出生時，支配那一年的動物，應該會對此人的命運有很大的影響。為了要有好運，人們在處理像是選丈夫或妻子這樣的重大事件時，就會注意生肖。

rule〔rul〕v. 支配　　influence〔'ɪnfluəns〕n. 影響

fate〔fet〕n. 命運　　luck〔lʌk〕n. 運氣

look to 留心；注意　　event〔ɪ'vɛnt〕n. 事件

choose〔tʃuz〕v. 選擇

3. (**F**) 依句意，當一個人出生時，支配那一年的動物，「應該」會對此人的命運有很大的影響，選 (F) ***supposed***。

suppose〔sə'poz〕v. 認為應該

be supposed to V. 應該…

4. (**A**) 人們在「處理」像是選丈夫或妻子這樣的重大事件時，就會
注意生肖，選 (A) *dealing*。　　*deal with*　處理

5. (**D**) 依句意，選 (D) *such as*「像是」(= *like*)。

Take a Goat woman for example. The Snake man is said to make the best spouse for her, [6](H) while marrying a Dog man might lead to an unhappy marriage. In addition, one has the [7](B) characteristics of the animal ruling his birth.

以屬羊的女人為例。據說屬蛇的男人對她來說，是最好的配偶，而嫁給屬狗的男人，則可能會導致婚姻不幸福。此外，每個人都會有支配他出生年的那種動物的特質。

> goat〔got〕*n.* 山羊　　*be said to*　據說
> spouse〔spauz〕*n.* 配偶　　marry〔'mærɪ〕*v.* 和…結婚
> *lead to*　導致　　unhappy〔ʌn'hæpɪ〕*adj.* 不幸的
> marriage〔'mærɪdʒ〕*n.* 婚姻　　*in addition*　此外
> birth〔bɜθ〕*n.* 出生

6. (**H**) 表對比、對照，須用 *while*「然而」。

7. (**B**) 依句意，每個人都會有支配他出生年的那種動物的「特質」，
選 (B) *characteristics*〔͵kærɪktə'rɪstɪks〕*n. pl.* 特質。

A person born in the year of the Rabbit, for instance, should be "sweet and gentle but timid." It seems that certain Chinese signs have bad and nasty [8](I) images in Western culture.

例如，在兔年出生的人，應該是「親切、溫柔，但卻膽小的」。在西方文化中，某些中國生肖似乎有不好的，或令人討厭的形象。

for instance 例如　　sweet〔swit〕*adj.* 親切的；和藹的

gentle〔'dʒɛntl̩〕*adj.* 溫和的；溫柔的

timid〔'tɪmɪd〕*adj.* 膽小的　　seem〔sim〕*v.* 似乎

certain〔'sɜtn̩〕*adj.* 某些

Chinese sign 生肖（= *animal sign*）

nasty〔'næstɪ〕*adj.* 令人討厭的　　Western〔'wɛstən〕*adj.* 西洋的

8. (**I**)　依句意，某些生肖似乎有不好的，或令人討厭的「形象」，
選 (I) *images*〔'ɪmɪdʒz〕*n. pl.* 形象。

For Westerners, a rat is someone who [9](G) tricks others out of their money and a pig is a dirty and greedy person. However, both animals are [10](C) respected: the Rat for its creativity and the Pig for its intelligence.

對西方人來說，老鼠是指會騙別人錢的人，而豬是指骯髒而且貪心的人。
但是，這兩種動物也同樣受人尊敬：因為老鼠有創意，而豬很聰明。

Westerner〔'wɛstənə〕*n.* 西方人

dirty〔'dɜtɪ〕*adj.* 髒的　　greedy〔'gridɪ〕*adj.* 貪心的

creativity〔ˌkrie'tɪvətɪ〕*n.* 創意；創造力

intelligence〔ɪn'tɛlədʒəns〕*n.* 聰明；智慧

9. (**G**)　老鼠是指會「騙」別人錢的人，選 (G) *tricks*。
trick〔trɪk〕*v.* 欺騙　　*trick sb. out of*… 騙取某人的…

10. (**C**)　但是，這兩種動物也同樣受人「尊敬」，選 (C) *respected*。
respect〔rɪ'spɛkt〕*v.* 尊敬

TEST 27

說明： 第 1 至 10 題，每題一個空格。請依文意在文章後所提供的 (A) 到 (J) 選項中分別選出最適當者。

　　For most dog owners, the expression "work like a dog" doesn't make much sense. But some dogs indeed perform very ___1___ jobs for much of their lives. They are guide dogs. Guide dogs help blind or ___2___ impaired people get around in the world. In most countries, they are allowed anywhere that the public is allowed: ___3___, it is an offense to ___4___ guide dogs access to taxis and restaurants. To help their handlers get where they want to go, obedience is the trait guide dogs must have; ___5___, guide dogs must know to disobey a command that would put their handlers in danger. This ability, called ___6___ disobedience, is perhaps the most amazing thing about guide dogs — that they can ___7___ obedience with their own assessment of the situation. This ___8___ is extremely important at crosswalks, ___9___ the handler and dog must work very closely together to navigate the situation safely. The success of the cooperation lies in a unique relationship. The successful handler-guide dog partnership is truly a team, reinforced continually by ___10___ from both partners. Guide dogs can make a dramatic change in the lives of their handlers. Without exception, the owners of guide dogs all embrace their newfound independence and have far richer and more productive lives. 【北模】

(A) visually   (B) affection   (C) nevertheless

(D) where   (E) deny   (F) capacity

(G) balance   (H) in fact   (I) selective

(J) demanding

TEST 27 詳解

For most dog owners, the expression "work like a dog" doesn't make much sense. But some dogs indeed perform very [1](J) demanding jobs for much of their lives. They are guide dogs.

對大多數的狗主人來說，「像條狗一樣工作（拼命工作）」這個說法，沒有多大的意義。但是某些狗，一生中絕大部分的時間，確實是在做很辛苦的工作。牠們就是導盲犬。

> owner〔'onɚ〕 *n.* 主人；擁有人
> expression〔ɪk'sprɛʃən〕 *n.* 說法；措辭　　***work like a dog*** 拼命工作
> ***make sense*** 有意義　　indeed〔ɪn'did〕 *adv.* 的確；眞正地
> perform〔pɚ'fɔrm〕 *v.* 做（工作）；執行（任務）
> much〔mʌtʃ〕 *pron.* 大量；許多　　guide〔gaɪd〕 *n.* 引導者
> ***guide dog*** 導盲犬

1. (**J**) ***demanding***〔dɪ'mændɪŋ〕 *adj.* 辛苦的；苛求的

Guide dogs help blind or [2](A) visually impaired people get around in the world. In most countries, they are allowed anywhere that the public is allowed: [3](H) in fact, it is an offense to [4](E) deny guide dogs access to taxis and restaurants.

導盲犬能幫助盲人或視力受損的人，在世界各地走動。在大多數的國家，群眾可以進入的地方，導盲犬都可以進入：事實上，不讓導盲犬上計程車，或進入餐館，是犯法的。

> blind〔blaɪnd〕 *adj.* 瞎的；失明的
> impaired〔ɪm'pɛrd〕 *adj.* 受損的　　***get around*** 到處走
> allow〔ə'laʊ〕 *v.* 允許…進入　　***the public*** 一般大衆
> offense〔ə'fɛns〕 *n.* 犯法行爲　　access〔'æksɛs〕 *n.* 接近；進入

2. (**A**) 導盲犬能幫助盲人或「視力」受損的人，在世界各地走動，
選 (A) *visually* (ˈvɪʒuəlɪ) *adv.* 視力上。

3. (**H**) *in fact* 事實上 (= *in reality* = *in truth* = *actually* =
as a matter of fact)

4. (**E**) 依句意，「不」讓導盲犬上計程車，或進入餐館是犯法的，
選 (E) *deny* (dɪˈnaɪ) *v.* 拒絕；不給予。
deny…access to～ 不讓…進入～

To help their handlers get where they want to go, obedience is the
trait guide dogs must have; [5](C) nevertheless, guide dogs must know
to disobey a command that would put their handlers in danger.

為了幫助使用導盲犬的人到他們想去的地方，導盲犬一定要有服從這個特
性；然而，導盲犬也必須要懂得反抗，任何會讓使用者有危險的命令。

handler (ˈhændlɚ) *n.* 操作者
obedience (əˈbidɪəns) *n.* 服從
trait (tret) *n.* 特色；特性
disobey (ˌdɪsəˈbe) *v.* 不服從；反抗
command (kəˈmænd) *n.* 命令　　danger (ˈdendʒɚ) *n.* 危險
put sb. in danger 使某人有危險

5. (**C**) *nevertheless* (ˌnɛvɚðəˈlɛs) *adv.* 然而

This ability, called [6](I) selective disobedience, is perhaps the most
amazing thing about guide dogs —— that they can [7](G) balance
obedience with their own assessment of the situation.

這種能力叫作選擇性的反抗，這也許是導盲犬最令人驚訝的地方——牠們
可以自己評估狀況，來衡量是否要服從。

ability〔ə'bɪlətɪ〕*n.* 能力　　disobedience〔͵dɪsə'bidɪəns〕*n.* 反抗
perhaps〔pɚ'hæps〕*adv.* 或許　amazing〔ə'mezɪŋ〕*adj.* 令人驚訝的
assessment〔ə'sɛsmənt〕*n.* 評估　　situation〔͵sɪtʃu'eʃən〕*n.* 狀況

6. (**I**) 依句意，這種能力叫作「選擇性的」反抗，選 (I) *selective*
　　〔sə'lɛktɪv〕*adj.* 選擇性的。

7. (**G**) *balance*〔'bæləns〕*v.* 衡量（兩個事物的）輕重

This ⁸**(F) capacity** is extremely important at crosswalks, ⁹**(D) where**
the handler and dog must work very closely together to navigate
the situation safely.　The success of the cooperation lies in a unique
relationship.

在遇到行人穿越道時，這種能力非常重要，使用者和狗，必須要非常密切
地合作，才能安全地橫越。合作要成功，就在於一種獨特的關係。

extremely〔ɪk'strimlɪ〕*adv.* 非常地
crosswalk〔'krɔs͵wɔk〕*n.* 行人穿越道
work together 合作　　closely〔'kloslɪ〕*adv.* 密切地
navigate〔'nɛvə͵get〕*v.* 駕駛；操縱；指引
navigate the situation safely 字面的意思是「安全地指引此情況」，
　　在此指「安全地橫越」。　　safely〔'seflɪ〕*adv.* 安全地
success〔sək'sɛs〕*n.* 成功　　cooperation〔ko͵ɑpə'reʃən〕*n.* 合作
lie in 在於　　unique〔ju'nik〕*adj.* 獨特的
relationship〔rɪ'leʃən͵ʃɪp〕*n.* 關係

8. (**F**) *capacity*〔kə'pæsətɪ〕*n.* 能力

9. (**D**) 表「地點」，關係副詞須用 *where*。

The successful handler-guide dog partnership is truly a team, reinforced continually by [10](B) affection from both partners.　Guide dogs can make a dramatic change in the lives of their handlers.

合作無間的使用者與導盲犬，其實就是一個團隊，而且藉由兩個夥伴之間的情感，可以不斷強化合作關係。導盲犬會讓使用者的人生有很大的改變。

> successful (sək'sɛsfəl) *adj.* 成功的
> partnership ('pɑrtnɚˏʃɪp) *n.* 合作；合作關係
> truly ('trulɪ) *adv.* 真正地；實在地　　team (tim) *n.* 團隊
> reinforce (ˏriɪn'fors) *v.* 強化
> continually (kən'tɪnjʊəlɪ) *adv.* 不斷地
> partner ('pɑrtnɚ) *n.* 夥伴　　dramatic (drə'mætɪk) *adj.* 重大的
> ***make a dramatic change*** 做了一個重大的改變

10. (**B**) ***affection*** (ə'fɛkʃən) *n.* 情感

Without exception, the owners of guide dogs all embrace their newfound independence and have far richer and more productive lives.

毫無例外地，導盲犬的主人全都很高興，能擁有他們新發現的獨立自主，還有更加豐富，而且更有生產力的人生。

> exception (ɪk'sɛpʃən) *n.* 例外
> ***without exception*** 無例外地
> embrace (ɪm'bres) *v.* 欣然接受；很高興能有
> newfound ('njʊ'faʊnd) *adj.* 新發現的
> independence (ˏɪndɪ'pɛndəns) *n.* 獨立自主
> rich (rɪtʃ) *adj.* 豐富的　　***far richer*** 更加豐富的
> productive (prə'dʌktɪv) *adj.* 有生產力的

TEST 28

說明： 第 1 至 10 題，每題一個空格。請依文意在文章後所提供的 (A) 到 (J) 選項中分別選出最適當者。

    Children the world over take a great delight in visiting the zoo. Many zoos have a section   1   especially for children, where they can pet rabbits, ducks, and other gentle animals. The children do this, however, at their own   2 . Even rabbits can be dangerous at times. Several years ago a rabbit bit a child on the finger;   3 , part of the finger had to be amputated. Strangely   4 , the child didn't seem to mind. He said he was probably the only person in the world to have had his finger   5   off by a rabbit.

    Animals are not the only interesting features of zoos. The people that go to visit zoos are fascinating in their own   6 . Zoo officials frequently complain that people seem to be unable to read signs. They insist   7   feeding the animals even when signs   8   are prominently posted. Such people, however, are not

deliberately trying to be disobedient. They are ___9___
trying to be kind. Of course, if they really had the best
interests of the animals in mind, they would refrain
___10___ feeding them. By feeding an animal the
wrong kind of food, one could literally kill it with
kindness. 【台中一中複習考】

(A) as a result   (B) to the contrary   (C) from
(D) on   (E) risk   (F) right
(G) bitten   (H) designed   (I) merely
(J) enough

TEST 28 詳解

Children the world over take a great delight in visiting the zoo.
Many zoos have a section [1](H) designed especially for children,
where they can pet rabbits, ducks, and other gentle animals.

全世界的小孩都很喜歡參觀動物園。許多動物園都有特別為兒童設計
的區域，孩子們可以在這些區域撫摸兔子、鴨子，和其他溫和的動物。

delight〔dɪ'laɪt〕*n.* 喜悅；歡喜
take delight in 喜歡　　　section〔'sɛkʃən〕*n.* 區域
especially〔ə'spɛʃəlɪ〕*adv.* 特別地
pet〔pɛt〕*v.* 撫摸　　duck〔dʌk〕*n.* 鴨子
gentle〔'dʒɛntl̩〕*adj.* 溫和的

1. (**H**) 依句意，許多動物園都有特別為兒童「設計」的區域，選 (H)
　　designed。　　design〔dɪ'zaɪn〕*v.* 設計

The children do this, however, at their own [2](E) risk. Even rabbits can
be dangerous at times. Several years ago a rabbit bit a child on the
finger; [3](A) as a result, part of the finger had to be amputated.

但是孩子們做這些動作時，後果要自行負責。有時候甚至連兔子都是危險
的。幾年前，有隻兔子咬了小孩的手指；結果部份的手指必須要被切除。

at times 有時候（ = *sometimes* ）
several〔'sɛvərəl〕*adj.* 幾個的
bite〔baɪt〕*v.* 咬（三態變化為：bite-bit-bitten）
finger〔'fɪŋgɚ〕*n.* 手指　　amputate〔'æmpjə,tet〕*v.* 切除；鋸掉

2. (**E**) 依句意,但是孩子們做這些動作時,後果要「自行負責」,
選 (E) *risk*。　　**at one's own risk** 自行負責

3. (**A**) 依句意,「結果」部份的手指必須要被切除,選 (A) *as a result*
「結果」。

Strangely [4](**J**) enough, the child didn't seem to mind. He said he
was probably the only person in the world to have had his finger
[5](**G**) bitten off by a rabbit.

奇怪的是,這個孩子似乎並不在意。他說他可能是世界上,唯一一個被
兔子咬斷手指的人。

　　strangely ('strendʒlɪ) *adv.* 奇怪地;奇怪的是
　　seem (sim) *v.* 似乎　　mind (maɪnd) *v.* 介意

4. (**J**) 依句意,「奇怪的是」,這個孩子似乎並不在意,選 (J) *enough*。
strangely enough 奇怪的是 (= *strangely*)

5. (**G**) 依句意,他說他可能是世界上,唯一一個被兔子「咬」斷
手指的人,選 (G) *bitten*。　　**bite off** 咬掉;咬下

　　Animals are not the only interesting features of zoos. The
people that go to visit zoos are fascinating in their own [6](**F**) right.
Zoo officials frequently complain that people seem to be unable to
read signs.

　　動物並不是動物園裡唯一有趣的東西。有<u>些</u>參<u>觀</u>動物園的人本身，就很吸引人。動物園的工作人員經常抱怨說，人們似乎看不懂告示。

> feature〔'fitʃɚ〕*n.* 特色；特別吸引人的東西
> fascinating〔'fæsn̩ˌetɪŋ〕*adj.* 吸引人的
> official〔ə'fɪʃəl〕*n.* 行政人員
> frequently〔'frikwəntlɪ〕*adv.* 經常
> complain〔kəm'plen〕*v.* 抱怨　　***be unable to V.*** 無法…
> read〔rid〕*v.* 看懂　　sign〔saɪn〕*n.* 告示

6. **(F)** ***in one's own right*** 本身；憑自己（生來）的權力（能力、
　　　價值等）

They insist [7]**(D) on** feeding the animals even when signs [8]**(B) to the** <u>contrary</u> are prominently posted.　Such people, however, are not deliberately trying to be disobedient.　They are [9]**(I)** <u>merely</u> trying to be kind.

甚至儘管告示就貼在很顯眼的地方，人們還是堅持要餵那些動物。但是這些人並不是故意要違規的。他們只是想要親切一點。

> insist〔ɪn'sɪst〕*v.* 堅持　　feed〔fid〕*v.* 餵
> prominently〔'prɑmənəntlɪ〕*adv.* 顯眼地
> post〔post〕*v.* 張貼
> deliberately〔dɪ'lɪbərɪtlɪ〕*adv.* 故意地
> disobedient〔ˌdɪsə'bidɪənt〕*adj.* 不聽話的；不服從的
> ***try to V.*** 想要…　　kind〔kaɪnd〕*adj.* 親切的；好心的

7. (**D**) *insist on* 堅持

8. (**B**) 依句意，甚至「儘管」告示就貼在很顯眼的地方，
選 (B) *to the contrary*「儘管」。

9. (**I**) 依句意，他們「只是」想要親切一點，選 (I) *merely* ('mɪrlɪ)
adv. 僅僅；只是。

Of course, if they really had the best interests of the animals in mind,
they would refrain **10**(C) from feeding them. By feeding an animal the
wrong kind of food, one could literally kill it with kindness.

當然，如果他們真心為了這些動物好，就會克制自己，不要餵牠們吃東西。
因為餵錯食物的話，他們的好意可能真的會殺死那隻動物。

interests ('ɪntrɪsts) *n. pl.* 利益；福利
mind (maɪnd) *n.* 心；精神
have…in mind 記住；把…記在心裡
refrain (rɪ'fren) *v.* 抑制；忍住
kind (kaɪnd) *n.* 種類
literally ('lɪtərəlɪ) *adv.* 真正地；確實地
kill (kɪl) *v.* 殺死
kindness ('kaɪndnɪs) *n.* 好意；親切的行為

10. (**C**) *refrain from* + *V-ing* 克制自己不要～
註：from 在此引申為表示「禁止；使…不能」的意思，常與此類
意義的動詞連用，例如 prohibit（禁止），refrain（抑制），
keep（阻止），prevent（阻止），hinder（阻礙），inhibit
（阻止），stop（阻止），deter（阻止）等。

TEST 29

說明： 第 1 至 10 題，每題一個空格。請依文意在文章後所提供的 (A) 到
(J) 選項中分別選出最適當者。

Visiting the Heian Shrine in Kyoto was an experience
that Kevin will never forget. Because he had ___1___
arrived in Japan and knew little about the people and
culture, he took a trip to this famous shrine to satisfy
his interest and curiosity. In the garden surrounding the
shrine, he ___2___ a small teahouse hidden under some
maple trees. Thinking that some tea would be ___3___,
he entered the tiny little house. Inside, a small, graceful
woman ___4___ motioned for him to sit nearest the
person serving the tea. Without his knowing it, the
___5___ had given Kevin the seat of honor, which meant
he was to be the ___6___ for all the other guests. Kevin
received a cup from the server and found the tea to be
very thick, green, and bitter — not at all what he had
___7___. Not knowing what to do, he held the cup for
a long time ___8___ to see what the others would do.

The others, however, were watching him since he was, unknowingly, the leader! He finally just smelled the tea and passed it to the person next to him. In his ___9___, Kevin felt he had ruined the ceremony for the other guests. Kevin decided never again to enter into such a serious gathering in a different ___10___ without first studying it. It was not his cup of tea. 【94 研究試卷】

(A) culture   (B) discovered   (C) expected

(D) hostess   (E) ignorance   (F) leader

(G) politely   (H) recently   (I) refreshing

(J) waiting

TEST 29 詳解

Visiting the Heian Shrine in Kyoto was an experience that Kevin will never forget. Because he had **[1](H) recently** arrived in Japan and knew little about the people and culture, he took a trip to this famous shrine to satisfy his interest and curiosity.

凱文永遠都不會忘記，參觀京都平安神宮的經歷。因爲他最近才到日本去，所以對這個民族和文化所知甚少，爲了滿足自己的興趣和好奇心，他來到這個著名的神社遊覽。

shrine〔ʃraɪn〕*n.*（日本的）神社　　Kyoto〔'kjoto〕*n.* 京都
experience〔ɪk'spɪrɪəns〕*n.* 經驗
arrive〔ə'raɪv〕*v.* 到達　　people〔'pipḷ〕*n.* 民族
culture〔'kʌltʃɚ〕*n.* 文化　　trip〔trɪp〕*n.* 旅行
satisfy〔'sætɪs,faɪ〕*v.* 滿足　　interest〔'ɪntrɪst〕*n.* 興趣
curiosity〔,kjʊrɪ'ɑsətɪ〕*n.* 好奇心

1. (**H**) *recently*〔'risṇtlɪ〕*adv.* 最近

In the garden surrounding the shrine, he **[2](B) discovered** a small teahouse hidden under some maple trees. Thinking that some tea would be **[3](I) refreshing**, he entered the tiny little house.

在環繞神社的庭園中，他發現了一個隱藏在楓樹下的小茶館。他想說喝點茶可以提神，所以就走進了那個很小的屋子。

surround〔sə'raʊnd〕*v.* 圍繞
teahouse〔'ti,haʊs〕*n.* 茶館
hide〔haɪd〕*v.* 隱藏（三態變化爲：hide-hid-hidden）
maple〔'mepḷ〕*n.* 楓樹　　tiny〔'taɪnɪ〕*adj.* 極小的

2. (**B**) 依句意，他「發現」了一個隱藏在楓樹下的小茶館，選 (B) ***discovered*** 。　discover〔dɪ'skʌvɚ〕*v.* 發現

3. (**I**) ***refreshing***〔rɪ'frɛʃɪŋ〕*adj.* 提神的

Inside, a small, graceful woman ⁴**(G) politely** motioned for him to sit nearest the person serving the tea. Without his knowing it, the ⁵**(D) hostess** had given Kevin the seat of honor, which meant he was to be the ⁶**(F) leader** for all the other guests.

裡面有個嬌小而優雅的女士，她很有禮貌地指示，要他坐在最靠近上茶的人的位置。他並不知道，女主人給他的是貴賓席，意思是他將成為其他所有客人的領袖。

> inside〔'ɪn'saɪd〕*adv.* 在裡面；在屋內
> graceful〔'gresfəl〕*adj.* 優雅的
> motion〔'moʃən〕*v.* 以手勢或動作指示
> serve〔sɝv〕*v.* 供應；端出　　knowing〔'noɪŋ〕*n.* 知道
> honor〔'ɑnɚ〕*n.* 光榮；尊敬　　***seat of honor*** 貴賓席
> mean〔min〕*v.* 意思是
> guest〔gɛst〕*n.* 客人

4. (**G**) 依句意，她很「有禮貌地」指示，選 (G) ***politely***〔pə'laɪtlɪ〕*adv.* 有禮貌地。

5. (**D**) ***hostess***〔'hostɪs〕*n.* 女主人

6. (**F**) 他將成為其他所有客人的「領袖」，選 (F) ***leader*** 。

Kevin received a cup from the server and found the tea to be very thick, green, and bitter — not at all what he had [7](C) expected. Not knowing what to do, he held the cup for a long time [8](J) waiting to see what the others would do.

凱文從服務生手上接過來一杯茶，然後他發現茶很濃、很綠，而且很苦——完全不是他所預期的那種。他不知道該怎麼做，所以有很長一段時間，他都一直拿著杯子，等著看看別人會怎麼做。

receive〔rɪ'siv〕v. 接受　　server〔'sɜvɚ〕n. 服務生
thick〔θɪk〕adj. 濃的　　bitter〔'bɪtɚ〕adj. 苦的
not at all 一點也不
hold〔hold〕v. 拿住；握著

7. (**C**) 依句意，完全不是他所「預期」的那種，選 (C) ***expected***。
　　　expect〔ɪk'spɛkt〕v. 預期

8. (**J**) 他都一直拿著杯子，「等著」看看別人會怎麼做，選 (J) ***waiting***。

The others, however, were watching him since he was, unknowingly, the leader! He finally just smelled the tea and passed it to the person next to him. In his [9](E) ignorance, Kevin felt he had ruined the ceremony for the other guests.

但是其他人都看著他，因為他已經不知不覺地成了領袖！最後他只有聞聞那杯茶，然後就把它傳給旁邊的人。凱文覺得對其他客人來說，他的無知破壞了這個儀式。

since〔sɪns〕conj.　因為
unknowingly〔ʌn'noɪŋlɪ〕adv. 不知不覺地
finally〔'faɪnlɪ〕adv. 最後

smell〔smɛl〕v. 聞　　pass〔pæs〕v. 傳遞

next to 在～旁邊的　　in〔ɪn〕*prep.* 因為

ruin〔'ruɪn〕v. 破壞　　ceremony〔'sɛrə,monɪ〕*n.* 儀式

9. (**E**) 凱文覺得對其他客人來說，他的「無知」破壞了這個儀式，

選 (E) ***ignorance***〔'ɪgnərəns〕*n.* 無知。

Kevin decided never again to enter into such a serious gathering in a different [10](A) culture without first studying it. It was not his cup of tea.

凱文決定，在沒有事先研究過一個不同的文化之前，再也不要參加像這樣嚴肅的聚會。他不喜歡這樣。

never again 再也不

enter into 參加　　serious〔'sɪrɪəs〕*adj.* 嚴肅的

gathering〔'gæðərɪŋ〕*n.* 聚會

different〔'dɪfərənt〕*adj.* 不同的

first〔fɜst〕*adv.* 先　　study〔'stʌdɪ〕v. 研究

one's cup of tea 喜愛的東西【這個片語通常用於否定句，源自英國人對茶的喜愛，英國還有一句話說：I wouldn't do it for all the tea in China. 字面意思是「就算你把全中國的茶都給我，我也不做這件事。」引申為「無論如何，我都不做這件事。」】

10. (**A**) 根據句意，在沒有事先研究過一個不同的「文化」之前，

選 (A) ***culture***。

TEST 30

說明：第 1 至 10 題，每題一個空格。請依文意在文章後所提供的 (A) 到 (J) 選項中分別選出最適當者。

In some cultures, parents are responsible for arranging marriages for their children. In ancient India, the marriage ___1___ was chosen by the parents together. If a young woman's parents had been ___2___ to find a husband three years after she had reached puberty, she could then arrange a marriage for herself. But by doing so, she would ___3___ great disgrace on her family. Likewise, in old Chinese society, a family elder was responsible for finding a husband for any young woman belonging to his household. The ___4___ decision on a prospective husband was typically made by the young woman's father. On the other hand, the mother would ___5___ her son's future wife. In modern Japan, the system of arranged marriage is somewhat similar to blind dating in the United States. When a young woman reaches ___6___ age, she and her parents compile a packet of information about her, including a photograph of her and

a   7   of her family background, education, hobbies,

accomplishments, and interests. Her parents then   8

among their friends and acquaintances to see if anyone

knows a man who would be a suitable husband for her.

The person who becomes the   9   shows the packet to

the potential bridegroom, and, if both parties are   10   ,

arranges a meeting between them. It is not uncommon

for a woman to have 10 or more such introductions before

she finds the man she wants to marry. 【94 研究試卷】

(A) select   (B) unable   (C) final

(D) bring   (E) matchmaker   (F) partner

(G) inquire   (H) description   (I) interested

(J) marriageable

TEST 30 詳解

In some cultures, parents are responsible for arranging marriages for their children. In ancient India, the marriage [1](F) partner was chosen by the parents together.

在某些文化中，父母要負責替孩子安排婚姻。在古印度，結婚的配偶是由父母一起選的。

culture〔ˈkʌltʃɚ〕 *n.* 文化
responsible〔rɪˈspɑnsəbḷ〕 *adj.* 負責的
arrange〔əˈrendʒ〕 *v.* 安排　　marriage〔ˈmærɪdʒ〕 *n.* 婚姻；結婚
ancient〔ˈenʃənt〕 *adj.* 古代的　　India〔ˈɪndɪə〕 *n.* 印度

1.(**F**) 依句意，在古印度，結婚的「配偶」是由父母一起選的，選 (F)。partner 主要意思是指「同伴」，marriage partner 就是「配偶」。

If a young woman's parents had been [2](B) unable to find a husband three years after she had reached puberty, she could then arrange a marriage for herself. But by doing so, she would [3](D) bring great disgrace on her family.

如果一名年輕女子的父母，無法在她到達青春期後的三年內，替她找到丈夫，那麼她就可以自己安排婚姻。但是這樣做，會給家族帶來很大的恥辱。

husband〔ˈhʌzbənd〕 *n.* 丈夫　　reach〔ritʃ〕 *v.* 達到
puberty〔ˈpjubɚtɪ〕 *n.* 青春期　　disgrace〔dɪsˈgres〕 *n.* 恥辱；丟臉

2.(**B**) *be unable to V.* 無法~

3.(**D**) 但是這樣做，會給家族「帶來」很大的恥辱，選 (D) *bring*。

Likewise, in old Chinese society, a family elder was responsible
for finding a husband for any young woman belonging to his
household. The [4](C) final decision on a prospective husband was
typically made by the young woman's father.

同樣地，在中國古代社會中，家族的長輩也要替屬於他那個家族的任何一
位年輕女子找到丈夫。一般都是由年輕女子的父親，來做最後的決定，替
她選擇未來的丈夫。

likewise ('laɪk‚waɪz) *adv.* 同樣地
society (sə'saɪətɪ) *n.* 社會　　elder ('ɛldə) *n.* 長輩
belong (bə'lɔŋ) *v.* 屬於 < *to* >
household ('haʊs‚hold) *n.* 家族
decision (dɪ'sɪʒən) *n.* 決定
prospective (prə'spɛktɪv) *adj.* 未來的
typically ('tɪpɪklɪ) *adv.* 一般地

4. (**C**)　依句意，一般都是由年輕女子的父親，來做「最後的」決
定，選 (C) ***final*** ('faɪnḷ) *adj.* 最後的。

On the other hand, the mother would [5](A) select her son's future wife.
In modern Japan, the system of arranged marriage is somewhat
similar to blind dating in the United States.

另一方面，母親也會替兒子選未來的妻子。現在在日本，安排婚姻的方式，
有點類似美國的盲目約會。

on the other hand 另一方面　　future ('fjutʃə) *adj.* 未來的
modern ('modən) *adj.* 現代的　　Japan (dʒə'pæn) *n.* 日本
system ('sɪstəm) *n.* 方式　　somewhat ('sʌm‚hwɑt) *adv.* 有點

similar（ˈsɪmələ）*adj.* 類似的　　blind（blaɪnd）*adj.* 盲目的
dating（ˈdetɪŋ）*n.* 約會
blind dating 盲目的約會；陌生男女的約會；相親

5. (**A**) 母親也會替兒子「選」未來的妻子，選 (A) ***select***（səˈlɛkt）*v.*
挑選。

When a young woman reaches [6](**J**) marriageable age, she and her
parents compile a packet of information about her, including a
photograph of her and a [7](**H**) description of her family background,
education, hobbies, accomplishments, and interests.

當一名年輕女子到達適婚年齡，她和她的父母就會收集一小袋關於她的資
料，包括她的照片，還有一份說明書，說明她的家庭背景、教育程度、嗜
好、成就，和興趣。

compile（kəmˈpaɪl）*v.* 收集（資料）；**編輯**
packet（ˈpækɪt）*n.* 小袋　　including（ɪnˈkludɪŋ）*prep.* 包括
photograph（ˈfotəˌgræf）*n.* 照片
background（ˈbækˌgraʊnd）*n.* 背景
education（ˌɛdʒʊˈkeʃən）*n.* 教育程度　　hobby（ˈhɑbɪ）*n.* 嗜好
accomplishments（əˈkɑmplɪʃmənts）*n. pl.* 成就
interest（ˈɪntrɪst）*n.* 興趣

6. (**J**) ***marriageable***（ˈmærɪdʒəb!）*adj.* 適合結婚的

7. (**H**) ***description***（dɪˈskrɪpʃən）*n.* 說明書

Her parents then [8](**G**) inquire among their friends and acquaintances
to see if anyone knows a man who would be a suitable husband for
her.

然後她的父母就會去問朋友和熟人，看有沒有人認識適合當她丈夫的人。

　　acquaintance (ə'kwɛntəns) *n.* 認識的人；熟人
　　suitable ('sutəbl̩) *adj.* 適合的

8. (**G**) *inquire* (ɪn'kwaɪr) *v.* 詢問

The person who becomes the [9](E) matchmaker shows the packet to the potential bridegroom, and, if both parties are [10](I) interested, arranges a meeting between them. It is not uncommon for a woman to have 10 or more such introductions before she finds the man she wants to marry.

變成媒人的人，會把這袋資料給可能成為新郎的人看，然後如果雙方都有興趣，就會安排他們見面。在一名女子找到她要嫁的人之前，被這樣介紹十次以上的，並不罕見。

　　show sth. *to sb.* 把某物給某人看
　　potential (pə'tɛnʃəl) *adj.* 可能的
　　bridegroom ('braɪd,grum) *n.* 新郎
　　party ('pɑrtɪ) *n.* 一方；當事人　　meeting ('mitɪŋ) *n.* 會面
　　uncommon (ʌn'kɑmən) *adj.* 罕見的
　　introduction (,ɪntrə'dʌkʃən) *n.* 介紹
　　marry ('mærɪ) *v.* 結婚

9. (**E**) 變成「媒人」的人，會把這袋資料給可能成為新郎的人看，選 (E) *matchmaker* ('mætʃ,mekə) *n.* 媒人。

10. (**I**) 依句意，如果雙方都「有興趣」，選 (I) *interested*。

TEST 31

說明： 第 1 至 10 題，每題一個空格。請依文意在文章後所提供的 (A) 到
(J) 選項中分別選出最適當者。

　　You probably think you're still young and can easily
remember anything. But what about actually improving
your memory just by eating different kinds of foods?
A(n) ___1___ diet can not only help you stay ___2___
while studying for tests, but also increase your ___3___
over time.

　　Remember there are a few golden rules about eating
in general. First, don't ___4___ at lunchtime! A lunch
of more than one thousand calories will probably make
you sleepy an hour later. Second, ___5___ foods such
as lean meats, beans, and cereals are ___6___ for good
concentration. And eating foods high in vitamin C, such
as oranges and avocados, will help your body ___7___
iron. Soybeans and oily fish are some things that will
___8___ your brain as well as your body. Also, ginkgo
has been used for thousands of years to improve the

memory. Many teas __9__ ginkgo leaf extract; therefore, choose these drinks rather than sugary sodas if you want to improve blood circulation in the brain. Finally, coffee can give your brain a kick in the morning; however, a high level of caffeine will have the __10__ effect. You don't want to be sleepy when taking your test and then lie awake all night!

So, a good diet, along with lots of rest and daily exercise, will improve your memory and keep your brain working at its best. 【台中女中複習考】

(A) contain   (B) opposite   (C) alert
(D) pig out   (E) brain-power   (F) nourish
(G) iron-rich   (H) absorb   (I) essential
(J) brain-boosting

TEST 31　詳解

You probably think you're still young and can easily remember anything. But what about actually improving your memory just by eating different kinds of foods?

你可能會覺得你還年輕，所以可以輕易地記住任何事。但是你覺得只藉由吃不同種類的食物，就能真的增進記憶力這件事如何？

probably〔'prɑbəblɪ〕*adv.* 可能
What about～? ～如何？；～怎麼樣？
actually〔'æktʃuəlɪ〕*adv.* 真地；實際上
improve〔ɪm'pruv〕*v.* 增進；改善　　　memory〔'mɛmərɪ〕*n.* 記憶力

A **[1](J)** brain-boosting diet can not only help you stay **[2](C)** alert while studying for tests, but also increase your **[3](E)** brain-power over time.

增強腦力的飲食，不但可以在你準備考試時，使你保持警覺，而且經過一段時間之後，還可以使你的腦力增強。

diet〔'daɪət〕*n.* 飲食　　***not only…but also～*** 不但…，而且～
stay〔ste〕*v.* 保持　　increase〔ɪn'kris〕*v.* 增加
over time 經過一段時間之後（*= over a period of time*）

1. (**J**)　依句意，「增強腦力的」飲食，可以在你準備考試時，使你保持警覺，選 (J) ***brain-boosting***。
　　boost〔bust〕*v.* 提高；增強

2. (**C**)　依句意，不但可以在你準備考試時，使你保持「警覺」，選 (C) ***alert***〔ə'lɝt〕*adj.* 警覺的；敏捷的。

3. (**E**)　根據句意，而且經過一段時間之後，還可以使你的「腦力」增強，選 (E) ***brain-power***。

Remember there are a few golden rules about eating in general. First, don't ⁴(D) pig out at lunchtime! A lunch of more than one thousand calories will probably make you sleepy an hour later.

你要記住一些和吃有關的一般黃金法則。首先,午餐時不要大吃!超過一千卡的午餐,可能會使你在一小時後覺得想睡。

golden〔'goldn〕*adj.* 黃金的　　rule〔rul〕*n.* 規則;法則
in general　(置於名詞後) 一般的;大概的
lunchtime〔'lʌntʃ,taɪm〕*n.* 午餐時間　　calorie〔'kælərɪ〕*n.* 卡路里
sleepy〔'slipɪ〕*adj.* 想睡的　　later〔'letɚ〕*adv.* 以後

4. (**D**) 依句意,首先,午餐時不要「大吃」,選 (D) *pig out*「狼吞虎嚥地大吃」。

Second, ⁵(G) iron-rich foods such as lean meats, beans, and cereals are ⁶(I) essential for good concentration. And eating foods high in vitamin C, such as oranges and avocados, will help your body ⁷(H) absorb iron.

第二,富含鐵質的食物,像是瘦肉、豆類,和穀類,是擁有良好注意力所必須的。而且,吃維他命 C 含量高的食物,像是柳橙和酪梨,都有助於讓身體吸收鐵質。

such as 像是　　lean〔lin〕*adj.* 瘦的　　meat〔mit〕*n.* 肉
bean〔bin〕*n.* 豆子　　cereal〔'sɪrɪəl〕*n.* 穀類
concentration〔,kɑnsṇ'treʃən〕*n.* 專心;注意力
vitamin〔'vaɪtəmɪn〕*n.* 維他命
avocado〔,ævə'kɑdo〕*n.* 酪梨　　iron〔'aɪən〕*n.* 鐵

5. (**G**) 「富含鐵質的」食物,選 (G) *iron-rich*。
　　　　rich〔rɪtʃ〕*adj.* 含量豐富的

6. (**I**) 依句意,是擁有良好注意力所「必須的」,選 (I)
　　　　essential〔ə'sɛnʃəl〕*adj.* 必須的;不可或缺的。

7. (**H**) 依句意，都有助於你的身體「吸收」鐵質，選 (H) **absorb**
〔 əb'sɔrb 〕*v.* 吸收。

Soybeans and oily fish are some things that will **8(F) nourish** your
brain as well as your body. Also, ginkgo has been used for
thousands of years to improve the memory.

大豆和含油的魚，則是能滋養頭腦和身體的食物。還有，幾千年來，人
們都用銀杏來增進記憶力。

> soybean〔'sɔɪ'bin〕*n.* 大豆　　oily〔'ɔɪlɪ〕*adj.* 含油的
> brain〔bren〕*n.* 頭腦　　**as well as** 以及
> also〔'ɔlso〕*adv.* 此外
> ginkgo〔'gɪŋko〕*n.* 銀杏

8. (**F**) 大豆和含油的魚，則是能「滋養」頭腦和身體的食物，
選 (F) **nourish**〔'nɜʃ〕*v.* 滋養。

Many teas **9(A) contain** ginkgo leaf extract; therefore, choose these
drinks rather than sugary sodas if you want to improve blood
circulation in the brain.

很多茶都含有銀杏葉的萃取物；因此，如果你要促進腦中的血液循環，
就可以選擇這種飲料，而不是含糖的汽水。

> leaf〔lif〕*n.* 葉子　　extract〔'ɛkstrækt〕*n.* 抽取物；萃取物
> therefore〔'ðɛr,for〕*adv.* 因此
> choose〔tʃuz〕*v.* 選擇　　drink〔drɪŋk〕*n.* 飲料
> **rather than** 而不是
> sugary〔'ʃugərɪ〕*adj.* 含糖的　　soda〔'sodə〕*n.* 汽水
> blood〔blʌd〕*n.* 血液　　circulation〔,sɜkjə'leʃən〕*n.* 循環

9. (**A**) 根據句意，很多茶都「含有」銀杏葉的萃取物，選 (A) *contain*
〔 kən'ten 〕 *v.* 含有。

Finally, coffee can give your brain a kick in the morning; however,
a high level of caffeine will have the [10](B) opposite effect. You
don't want to be sleepy when taking your test and then lie awake
all night!

最後，早上喝咖啡可以刺激你的頭腦；但是，咖啡因含量高則會有反效果。
你不會想要在考試時想睡，然後整晚都十分清醒地躺著吧！

> finally〔'faɪnlɪ〕 *adv.* 最後　　coffee〔'kɔfɪ〕 *n.* 咖啡
> kick〔kɪk〕 *n.* 刺激　　level〔'lɛvl̩〕 *n.* 含量；濃度
> caffeine〔'kæfin〕 *n.* 咖啡因　　effect〔ɪ'fɛkt〕 *n.* 效果
> lie〔laɪ〕 *v.*（以…的狀態）躺著　　awake〔ə'wek〕 *adj.* 醒著的

10. (**B**) 依句意，咖啡因含量高則會有「反」效果，選 (B) *opposite*
〔'ɑpəzɪt〕 *adj.* 相反的。

So, a good diet, along with lots of rest and daily exercise, will
improve your memory and keep your brain working at its best.

所以，良好的飲食和大量的休息，還有每天運動，就會使你的記憶
力增強，並且讓你的頭腦保持在最佳狀態。

> diet〔'daɪət〕 *n.* 飲食
> *along with* 連同　　rest〔rɛst〕 *n.* 休息
> daily〔'delɪ〕 *adj.* 每天的　　exercise〔'ɛksə‚saɪz〕 *n.* 運動
> work〔wɝk〕 *v.* 運作
> *at one's best* 處於最佳狀態

TEST 32

說明： 第 1 至 10 題，每題一個空格。請依文意在文章後所提供的 (A) 到 (J) 選項中分別選出最適當者。

America encourages its young people to drink. ___1___, our society makes drinking a part of every celebration. Our personal celebrations such as weddings, promotions, graduations, and ___2___, are closely linked with drinking. Few children can attend any family affair without seeing the adults enjoying their ___3___. Drinking is part of our ___4___ celebrations as well. The Fourth of July means beer and New Year's Eve is an entire night dedicated to the proposition that everyone must get drunk. Secondly, the shows young people watch on television encourage them to drink. On almost every soap opera, the ___5___ drink casually and often. The rock videos young people watch over and over again ___6___ alcohol, too. Characters in the videos sit in bars, nightclubs, and roadhouses. Drinking,

the ___7___ goes, is cool. The strongest encouragement
to drink that young people receive, however, comes from
advertisers. Beer companies often ___8___ the sports
events young people watch. ___9___, advertisements
for liquor, on TV and in print, show situations that are
attractive to the young. People raise their ___10___
while they are sitting around ski lodges, sailing, dancing,
or enjoying a football game. We may say we don't
want our children to drink, but our messages say just
the opposite. 【93 研究試卷】

(A) liquor   (B) message   (C) feature

(D) glasses   (E) sponsor   (F) characters

(G) national   (H) anniversaries (I) In addition

(J) For one thing

TEST 32 詳解

America encourages its young people to drink. **[1](J) For one thing**, our society makes drinking a part of every celebration. Our personal celebrations such as weddings, promotions, graduations, and **[2](H) anniversaries**, are closely linked with drinking.

美國鼓勵年輕人喝酒。首先，我們的社會已經把喝酒變成每個慶祝活動的一部份。個人的慶祝，像是婚禮、升遷、畢業和週年紀念日，都和喝酒密切相關。

> encourage〔ɪn'kɝɪdʒ〕v. 鼓勵　　drink〔drɪŋk〕v. 喝；喝酒
> society〔sə'saɪətɪ〕n. 社會
> celebration〔,sɛlə'breʃən〕n. 慶祝活動；慶典
> personal〔'pɝsn̩l〕adj. 個人的　　*such as* 像是
> wedding〔'wɛdɪŋ〕n. 婚禮
> promotion〔prə'moʃən〕n. 升遷
> graduation〔,grædʒʊ'eʃən〕n. 畢業
> closely〔'kloslɪ〕adv. 密切地　　link〔lɪŋk〕v. 連結
> *be linked with* 與～有關
> drinking〔'drɪŋkɪŋ〕n. 喝酒

1. (**J**)　依句意，選 (J) *For one thing*「首先」。

2. (**H**) *anniversary*〔,ænə'vɝsərɪ〕n. 週年紀念日

Few children can attend any family affair without seeing the adults enjoying their **[3](A) liquor**. Drinking is part of our **[4](G) national** celebrations as well.

很少有小孩在參加任何家族活動時，不會看到大人開心地喝酒。喝酒也
是國家慶典的一部份。

> attend〔əˋtɛnd〕v. 參加；出席　　affair〔əˋfɛr〕n. 活動；慶典
> adult〔əˋdʌlt〕n. 成人　　enjoy〔ɪnˋdʒɔɪ〕v. 享受；快樂地品嚐
> *as well* 也；又

3. (**A**) 根據句意，很少有小孩在參加任何家族活動時，不會看到大人
　　　開心地喝「酒」，選 (A) *liquor*〔ˋlɪkɚ〕n. 酒。

4. (**G**) 喝酒也是「國家」慶典的一部份，選 (G) *national*〔ˋnæʃənl̩〕
　　　adj. 國家的。

The Fourth of July means beer and New Year's Eve is an entire
night dedicated to the proposition that everyone must get drunk.
Secondly, the shows young people watch on television encourage
them to drink.

七月四日（美國國慶）就意味著喝啤酒，還有除夕一整晚，每個人也都會
致力於一定要喝醉這件事。第二，年輕人看的電視節目，也鼓勵他們喝酒。

> mean〔min〕v. 意味著　　beer〔bɪr〕n. 啤酒
> *New Year's Eve* 除夕　　entire〔ɪnˋtaɪr〕*adj.* 整個的
> dedicate〔ˋdɛdəˌket〕v. 奉獻；致力於　　*be dedicated to* 致力於
> proposition〔ˌprɑpəˋzɪʃən〕n. 提議；事情
> drunk〔drʌŋk〕*adj.* 酒醉的　　secondly〔ˋsɛkəndlɪ〕*adv.* 第二；其次
> show〔ʃo〕n. 節目；表演

On almost every soap opera, the [5](F) characters drink casually and
often. The rock videos young people watch over and over again [6](C)
feature alcohol, too. Characters in the videos sit in bars, nightclubs,
and roadhouses.

幾乎在每部電視連續劇中，都很常看到劇中的角色不經意地喝著酒。在年輕人一再重複收看的搖滾樂的錄影帶中，酒也佔了很重要的地位。影片中的人物都坐在酒吧、夜總會和酒館裡。

> ***soap opera*** 電視連續劇；肥皂劇
> casually〔ˈkæʒʊəlɪ〕*adv.* 不經意地　　rock〔rɑk〕*adj.* 搖滾樂的
> video〔ˈvɪdɪˌo〕*n.* 錄影帶
> ***over and over again*** 一再地　　alcohol〔ˈælkəˌhɔl〕*n.* 酒
> character〔ˈkærɪktɚ〕*n.* (劇中的) 角色；人物
> bar〔bɑr〕*n.* 酒吧　　nightclub〔ˈnaɪtˌklʌb〕*n.* 夜總會
> roadhouse〔ˈrodˌhaʊs〕*n.* 酒館

5. (**F**) 幾乎在每部電視連續劇中，都很常看到「劇中的角色」不經意地喝著酒，選 (F) ***characters***。

6. (**C**) 依句意，在年輕人一再重複收看的搖滾樂的錄影帶中，酒也「佔了很重要的地位」，選 (C) ***feature***〔ˈfitʃɚ〕*v.* 佔重要地位。

Drinking, the [7](B) message goes, is cool. The strongest encouragement to drink that young people receive, however, comes from advertisers.

表達出的訊息是，喝酒很酷。然而，年輕人所受到的最大鼓勵，是來自刊登廣告的人。

> go〔go〕*v.* (訊息、話) 是…　　cool〔kul〕*adj.* 酷的；很棒的
> encouragement〔ɪnˈkɝɪdʒmənt〕*n.* 鼓勵　　receive〔rɪˈsiv〕*v.* 接受
> advertiser〔ˈædvɚˌtaɪzɚ〕*n.* 刊登廣告者

7. (**B**) 依句意，表達出的「訊息」是，喝酒很酷，選 (B) ***message***〔ˈmɛsɪdʒ〕*n.* 訊息；寓意。

Beer companies often [8](E) sponsor the sports events young people watch. [9](I) In addition, advertisements for liquor, on TV and in print, show situations that are attractive to the young.

啤酒公司常常贊助年輕人看的運動比賽。另外，在電視或印刷品上的酒類廣告，都會出現很吸引年輕人的場面。

> event〔ɪ'vɛnt〕*n.* 比賽項目
> advertisement〔͵ædvɚ'taɪzmənt〕*n.* 廣告　　print〔prɪnt〕*n.* 印刷品
> situation〔͵sɪtʃʊ'eʃən〕*n.* 情境；場面
> attractive〔ə'træktɪv〕*adj.* 吸引人的
> *the young* 年輕人 (= *young people*)

8. (**E**) 啤酒公司常常「贊助」年輕人看的運動比賽，選 (E) *sponsor*
　　　〔'spɑnsɚ〕*v.* 贊助。

9. (**I**) 「此外」，在電視或印刷品上的酒類廣告，選 (I) *In addition*。

People raise their [10](D) glasses while they are sitting around ski lodges, sailing, dancing, or enjoying a football game. We may say we don't want our children to drink, but our messages say just the opposite.

當人們坐在滑雪屋裡、航海、跳舞，或是看橄欖球賽時，都會乾杯。我們可能會說不想要孩子喝酒，但是我們表達出的訊息，卻正好相反。

> raise〔rez〕*v.* 舉起　　around〔ə'raʊnd〕*prep.* 在…四處
> lodge〔lɑdʒ〕*n.* 小屋　　sailing〔'selɪŋ〕*n.* 航海
> football〔'fʊt͵bɔl〕*n.* 橄欖球　　opposite〔'ɑpəzɪt〕*n.* 相反的東西

10. (**D**) *raise one's glass* 舉杯；乾杯

TEST 33

說明: 第 1 至 10 題，每題一個空格。請依文意在文章後所提供的 (A) 到 (J) 選項中分別選出最適當者。

Bill Gates, the software king, has made ___1___ possible for millions of people to travel freely in the computer world. Many people attribute his success ___2___ his remarkable personality. First, Bill Gates is so confident and highly intelligent that he ___3___ saw early the potential of the computer, but came up with a way to use the computer to make a great fortune. Besides, he is a very competitive and intense man. ___4___, he won his first fight with the U.S. government, ___5___ tried to break up Microsoft because it had become so powerful. Above all, Bill Gates is never completely satisfied with his achievements. He always ___6___ that his company will expand into new areas of technology ___7___ computers that can be operated by the human voice. ___8___ his focus on his work, Bill Gates is also a responsible and generous member of the global village. ___9___ giving computers to schools in poor neighborhoods and to small-town libraries, he donates large ___10___ of money to universities to support their research on the computer. For Bill Gates, the future is much more important than the past. 〔中正高中期中考〕

(A) In spite of (B) For instance (C) In addition to

(D) it (E) makes sure (F) not only

(G) such as (H) sums (I) to

(J) which

TEST 33 詳解

Bill Gates, the software king, has made **¹(D) it** possible for millions of people to travel freely in the computer world. Many people attribute his success **²(I) to** his remarkable personality.

比爾蓋茲是軟體之王，他讓數百萬人能自在地悠遊於電腦世界中。許多人把他的成功歸因於他與眾不同的個性。

> software〔'sɔft,wεr〕*n.* 軟體　　possible〔'pasəbḷ〕*adj.* 可能的
> million〔'mɪljən〕*n.* 百萬　　***millions of*** 數百萬的
> freely〔'frilɪ〕*adv.* 自由地
> attribute〔ə'trɪbjut〕*v.* 把…歸因於 < *to* >
> success〔sək'sεs〕*n.* 成功
> remarkable〔rɪ'markəbḷ〕*adj.* 非凡的；引人注目的
> personality〔,pɝsṇ'ælətɪ〕*n.* 個性；性格

1. (**D**) *it* 做虛主詞，代替其後眞正的主詞 to travel…world。

2. (**I**) *attribute* A *to* B 把 A 歸因於 B

   ⎧ attribute A to B
   ⎨ = owe A to B（通常指好的方面）
   ⎩ = ascribe A to B

First, Bill Gates is so confident and highly intelligent that he **³(F) not only** saw early the potential of the computer, but came up with a way to use the computer to make a great fortune.

首先，比爾蓋茲很有自信，而且非常聰明，他不但很早就看出電腦的潛力，還想出利用電腦發大財的方法。

confident ('kɑnfədənt) *adj.* 有自信的

highly ('haɪlɪ) *adv.* 非常

intelligent (ɪn'tɛlədʒənt) *adj.* 聰明的

potential (pə'tɛnʃəl) *n.* 潛力　　***come up with*** 想出

fortune ('fɔrtʃən) *n.* 財富

make a fortune 發財；賺大錢

3. (**F**) 依句意，他「不但」很早就看出電腦的潛力，「還」想出利用
電腦發大財的方法，選 (F) ***not only***。
not only⋯but also ~　不但⋯而且 ~

Besides, he is a very competitive and intense man. <u>⁴(B) For instance,</u>
<u>he won his first fight with the U.S. government, ⁵(J) which</u> tried to
break up Microsoft because it had become so powerful.

此外，他是個很喜歡競爭，而且很認真的人。舉例來說，他打贏了和美國
政府的第一場戰爭，美國政府試圖要解散微軟公司，因為該公司變得太
強大了。

besides (bɪ'saɪdz) *adv.* 此外

competitive (kəm'pɛtətɪv) *adj.* 好競爭的

intense (ɪn'tɛns) *adj.* 認真的　　win (wɪn) *v.* 贏

fight (faɪt) *n.* 戰爭

government ('gʌvənmənt) *n.* 政府

break up 解散　　powerful ('pauəfəl) *adj.* 強大的

4. (**B**) ***for instance*** 例如

5. (**J**) 空格應填關代，代替先行詞 the U.S. government，故選 (J)
which。

Above all, Bill Gates is never completely satisfied with his achievements. He always ⁶<u>(E) makes sure</u> that his company will expand into new areas of technology ⁷<u>(G) such as</u> computers that can be operated by the human voice.

最重要的是，比爾蓋茲從來不會很滿足於自己的成就。他總是想要確保公司會擴展到新的科技領域，像是能用人的聲音來操作的電腦。

> ***above all*** 最重要的是
> completely〔kəm'plitlɪ〕*adv.* 完全地；十分
> ***be satisfied with*** 對～感到滿足
> achievements〔ə'tʃivmənts〕*n. pl.* 成就
> expand〔ɪk'spænd〕*v.* 發展；擴展
> area〔'ɛrɪə〕*n.* 領域
> technology〔tɛk'nɑlədʒɪ〕*n.* 科技
> operate〔'ɑpə,ret〕*v.* 操作   voice〔vɔɪs〕*n.* 聲音

6. (**E**) 依句意，他總是想要「確定」公司會擴展到新的科技領域，選 (E) ***makes sure*** 「確定」。

7. (**G**) 「像是」能用人的聲音來操作的電腦，選 (G) ***such as***。

⁸<u>(A) In spite of</u> his focus on his work, Bill Gates is also a responsible and generous member of the global village.

儘管比爾蓋茲的注意力都集中在工作上，但他也是一位很負責任，而且很慷慨的地球村成員。

> focus〔'fokəs〕*n.* (注意力的) 焦點；集中點
> responsible〔rɪ'spɑnsəbḷ〕*adj.* 負責任的
> generous〔'dʒɛnərəs〕*adj.* 慷慨的

member (＇mɛmbɚ) *n.* 成員

global (＇globl̩) *adj.* 地球的　　village (＇vɪlɪdʒ) *n.* 村莊

8. (**A**)　「儘管」比爾蓋茲的注意力都集中在工作上，選 (A) *In spite of*。

⁹**(C) In addition to** giving computers to schools in poor

neighborhoods and to small-town libraries, he donates large

¹⁰**(H) sums** of money to universities to support their research on

the computer. For Bill Gates, the future is much more important

than the past.

除了送電腦給貧困地區的學校，還有小鎮的圖書館之外，他還捐贈一
大筆錢給大學，以支持他們在電腦方面的研究。對比爾蓋茲來說，未
來比過去重要多了。

poor (pur) *adj.* 貧窮的

neighborhood (＇nebɚ,hud) *n.* 地區；地方

town (taun) *n.* 小鎮　　library (＇laɪ,brɛrɪ) *n.* 圖書館

donate (＇donet) *v.* 捐贈

university (,junə＇vɝsətɪ) *n.* 大學

support (sə＇port) *v.* 支持

research (rɪ＇sɝtʃ , ＇risɝtʃ) *n.* 研究　　past (pæst) *n.* 過去

9. (**C**)「除了」送電腦給貧困地區的學校，還有小鎮的圖書館「之外」，
選 (C) *In addition to*「除了…之外」。

10. (**H**) 他還捐贈一大「筆」錢給學校，選 (H) *sums* (sʌmz) *n. pl.* 金額。

TEST 34

說明: 第 1 至 10 題，每題一個空格。請依文意在文章後所提供的 (A) 到
(J) 選項中分別選出最適當者。

Ralph Waldo Emerson, born on May 25, 1803 in
Boston, Massachusetts, is widely regarded as one of
America's most ___1___ authors, philosophers and
thinkers. At one time a Unitarian minister, Emerson
left his position because of doctrinal ___2___ with his
superiors. Soon after, on a trip to Europe, he met a
number of intellectuals, ___3___ Thomas Carlyle and
William Wordsworth. The ideas of these men, along
with ___4___ of Plato and some of the Hindu, Buddhist,
and Persian thinkers, strongly influenced his development
of the ___5___ of "Transcendentalism". In 1836, Emerson
expressed Transcendentalism's main principle of the "
___6___ unity of nature" in his essay, "Nature". Emerson
___7___ independent thinking and emphasized that not all
life's answers were found in books. In "The American
Scholar", his famous ___8___ to the Phi Beta Kappa

Society at Cambridge in 1837, Emerson stated that:
"Books are the best of things, well used; abused, __9__
the worst." He believed that a scholar learned best by
engaging life. His essays on "The Conduct of Life"
__10__ what one might do to engage life "skillfully."
Today, Emerson's works still enjoy an international
reputation. 【中正高中期中考】

    (A) mystical   (B) including   (C) among
    (D) outline   (E) disputes   (F) philosophy
    (G) influential   (H) those   (I) urged
    (J) address

TEST 34 詳解

Ralph Waldo Emerson, born on May 25, 1803 in Boston, Massachusetts, is widely regarded as one of America's most [1](G) influential authors, philosophers and thinkers.

拉爾夫·沃爾多·愛默生於一八○三年五月二十五日，出生於麻薩諸塞州的波士頓，大家普遍認為他是美國最有影響力的作家、哲學家，和思想家之一。

Boston〔'bɔstn̩〕*n.* 波士頓 (美國麻薩諸塞州的首府)
Massachusetts〔,mæsə'tʃusəts〕*n.* 麻薩諸塞州
widely〔'waɪdlɪ〕*adv.* 普遍地
regard〔rɪ'gɑrd〕*v.* 認為　　author〔'ɔðə〕*n.* 作家
philosopher〔fə'lɑsəfə〕*n.* 哲學家
thinker〔'θɪŋkə〕*n.* 思想家

1. (**G**) *influential*〔,ɪnflʊ'ɛnʃəl〕*adj.* 有影響力的

At one time a Unitarian minister, Emerson left his position because of doctrinal [2](E) disputes with his superiors. Soon after, on a trip to Europe, he met a number of intellectuals, [3](B) including Thomas Carlyle and William Wordsworth.

他曾擔任唯一教派的牧師，但因為和上司在教義上有爭論而離職。不久，他就到歐洲去旅行，並在途中認識了很多知識份子，包括湯瑪斯·卡萊爾，和威廉·渥茲華斯。

at one time 曾經　　Unitarian〔,junə'tɛrɪən〕*adj.* 唯一教派的
minister〔'mɪnɪstə〕*n.* 牧師　　position〔pə'zɪʃən〕*n.* 職位

doctrinal〔'dɑktrɪnḷ〕*adj.* 教義上的

superior〔sə'pɪrɪə〕*n.* 上司

soon after 不久之後　　Europe〔'jurəp〕*n.* 歐洲

a number of 許多的　　intellectual〔ˌɪntḷ'ɛktʃuəl〕*n.* 知識份子

2. (**E**) 依句意，但因為和上司在教義上有「爭論」，選 (E) ***disputes***。

　　dispute〔dɪ'spjut〕*n.* 爭論

3. (**B**) 依句意，認識了很多知識份子，「包括」湯瑪斯・卡萊爾，

　　和威廉・渥茲華斯，選 (B) ***including***。

The ideas of these men, along with [4](**H**) those of Plato and some of
the Hindu, Buddhist, and Persian thinkers, strongly influenced his
development of the [5](**F**) philosophy of "Transcendentalism".

這些人的思想，還有柏拉圖，以及一些印度教徒、佛教徒和波斯思想家
的想法，都對他的「超驗主義」哲學發展，有很大的影響。

along with 連同　　Plato〔'pleto〕*n.* 柏拉圖

Hindu〔'hɪndu〕*n.* 印度教徒　　Buddhist〔'budɪst〕*n.* 佛教徒

Persian〔'pɝʃən〕*adj.* 波斯的　　strongly〔'strɔŋlɪ〕*adv.* 強大地

influence〔'ɪnfluəns〕*v.* 影響

development〔dɪ'vɛləpmənt〕*n.* 發展

transcendentalism〔ˌtrænsɛn'dɛntḷˌɪzəm〕*n.* 超驗主義

4. (**H**) 為避免重覆前面提過的名詞，單數可用 that 代替，複數可用

　　those 代替，故選 (H) ***those***，在此等於 the ideas。

5. (**F**) 都對他的超驗主義「哲學」發展，有很大的影響，選 (F)

　　philosophy〔fə'lɑsəfɪ〕*n.* 哲學。

In 1836, Emerson expressed Transcendentalism's main principle of the " ⁶(A) mystical unity of nature" in his essay, "Nature". Emerson ⁷(I) urged independent thinking and emphasized that not all life's answers were found in books.

一八三六年時,愛默生在他的評論「論自然」中,陳述了超驗主義的主要信念,也就是「自然界的神秘和諧」。愛默生鼓勵獨立思考,而且還強調,並非所有關於生命的問題,都可以在書中找到答案。

> express〔ɪk'sprɛs〕v. 表達;陳述
> main〔men〕adj. 主要的
> principle〔'prɪnsəpl̩〕n. 原則;基本信念;信條
> unity〔'junətɪ〕n. 和諧   essay〔'ɛse〕n. 評論;小品文
> nature〔'netʃɚ〕n. 自然界
> independent〔ˌɪndɪ'pɛndənt〕adj. 獨立的
> ***independent thinking*** 獨立思考   emphasize〔'ɛmfə͵saɪz〕v. 強調

6. (**A**) 自然界的「神秘」和諧,選 (A) ***mystical***〔'mɪstɪkl̩〕adj. 神祕的。

7. (**I**) 依句意,愛默生「鼓勵」獨立思考,選 (I) ***urge***〔ɝdʒ〕v. 鼓勵;激勵。

In "The American Scholar", his famous ⁸(J) address to the Phi Beta Kappa Society at Cambridge in 1837, Emerson stated that: "Books are the best of things, well used; abused, ⁹(C) among the worst."

一八三七年時,他在劍橋對美國菁英學會發表了一篇著名的演說,即「論美國學者」,愛默生說到:「如果善用書,那麼書是最棒的東西;如果濫用,那它就會是最糟糕的東西。」

scholar〔'skɑlɚ〕*n.* 學者　　famous〔'feməs〕*adj.* 有名的

Phi Beta Kappa〔'faɪˌbetə'kæpə〕*n.* 菁英學會（1776 年創設，由
　成績優良的美國大學生、畢業生所組成的學會）

society〔sə'saɪətɪ〕*n.* 學會；團體

Cambridge〔'kembrɪdʒ〕*n.* 劍橋（美國麻薩諸塞州的一個城市）

state〔stet〕*v.* 敘述；說明　　abuse〔ə'bjuz〕*v.* 濫用

8. (**J**)　依句意，他在劍橋對美國菁英學會發表了一篇著名的「演說」，
　　　　選 (J) ***address***〔ə'drɛs〕*n.* 演說。

9. (**C**)　***among***〔ə'mʌŋ〕*prep.* 在…之中

He believed that a scholar learned best by engaging life.　His essays
on "The Conduct of Life" **¹⁰**(**D**) outline what one might do to engage
life "skillfully."　Today, Emerson's works still enjoy an international
reputation.

他認為藉由參與人生來學習的學者，可以學到最多東西。在他所寫的評
論「人生的行為」中，概述了一個人可能要做些什麼，才能「巧妙地」
參與人生。現在愛默生的作品依然享譽國際。

engage〔ɪn'gedʒ〕*v.* 參與（= *participate in*）

conduct〔'kɑndʌkt〕*n.* 行為

skillfully〔'skɪfəlɪ〕*adv.* 巧妙地　　today〔tə'de〕*adv.* 現今；現在

enjoy〔ɪn'dʒɔɪ〕*v.* 享有　　work〔wɝk〕*n.* 作品

international〔ˌɪntɚ'næʃənḷ〕*adj.* 國際上的

reputation〔ˌrɛpjə'teʃən〕*n.* 名聲；聲譽

10. (**D**)　依句意，在他所寫的評論「人生的行為」中，「概述」了一
　　　　個人可能要做些什麼，才能「巧妙地」參與人生，選 (D)
　　　　outline〔'aʊtˌlaɪn〕*v.* 概述。

TEST 35

說明： 第 1 至 10 題，每題一個空格。請依文意在文章後所提供的 (A) 到 (J) 選項中分別選出最適當者。

Pope John Paul was born in 1920 in Poland. He began his priestly training in 1942, in an underground seminary kept ___1___ from the Nazis; after his ordination, in 1946, he worked in a church in the then Communist Poland. Some of Pope John Paul's most ___2___ acts were speeches made to oppressed peoples, within earshot of their leaders, appealing to them to treasure their human rights and ___3___ any form of oppression. He did this in Chile, Cuba and the Philippines, as well as in his ___4___, Poland.

This was also a Pope who could spring surprises. As a Pope from a town full of Jews, he felt a special ___5___ to respect them and was the first Pope to push a folded prayer-note between the stones of the Wailing Wall in Jerusalem. In 2000, ___6___, he read out a long apology for the church's bad behavior over the centuries.

Some noted that it was church members, __7__ the church itself, for whom he apologized. __8__, it was a rare marvel that a man so certain of the church's possession of the truth should criticize those who had believed it with equal enthusiasm.

The greatest surprise, however, was the strength of spirit that kept him going. He carried on largely in order to __9__, to a cynical world, the power of God at work in him and the needlessness of the fear of death. __10__ he has passed away, his bruised and worried church feels, more than anything, the lack of his confidence.

【成功高中期末考】

(A) display   (B) Now that   (C) rise up against

(D) secret   (E) admirable   (F) startlingly

(G) Nonetheless   (H) obligation   (I) homeland

(J) not

TEST 35 詳解

Pope John Paul was born in 1920 in Poland. He began his priestly training in 1942, in an underground seminary kept **¹(D) secret** from the Nazis; after his ordination, in 1946, he worked in a church in the then Communist Poland.

教宗若望保祿二世於一九二○年，出生於波蘭。一九四二年時，他開始在地下神學院，接受神職訓練，神學院秘密運作是為了不讓納粹黨發現；在一九四六年的授聖職禮後，他就到教堂去工作，而該教堂是位於當時正施行共產主義的波蘭。

Pope〔pop〕*n.* 羅馬教宗 　 Poland〔'poland〕*n.* 波蘭
priestly〔'pristlı〕*adj.* 神職者的 　 training〔'trenıŋ〕*n.* 訓練
underground〔'ʌndə'graʊnd〕*adj.* 地下的；秘密的
seminary〔'sɛmə,nɛrı〕*n.* 天主教的神學院
Nazis〔'natsız〕*n. pl.* 納粹黨 　 ordination〔,ɔrdn̩'eʃən〕*n.* 授聖職禮
church〔tʃɜtʃ〕*n.* 教堂；教會 　 then〔ðɛn〕*adj.* 那時的；當時的
Communist〔'kamju,nıst〕*adj.* 共產主義的

1. (**D**) 依句意，神學院「秘密」運作是為了不讓納粹黨發現，選 (D)
 secret〔'sikrıt〕*adj.* 秘密的。

Some of Pope John Paul's most **²(E) admirable** acts were speeches made to oppressed peoples, within earshot of their leaders, appealing to them to treasure their human rights and **³(C) rise up against** any form of oppression.

教宗若望保祿二世最令人欽佩的行為，是對受壓迫的民族，所發表的演說，而且是在其領袖的聽力所及範圍內這樣做，他呼籲他們，要珍惜自己的人權，並反抗任何形式的壓迫。

> act〔ækt〕*n.* 行為　　speech〔spitʃ〕*n.* 演講
> oppressed〔ə'prɛst〕*adj.* 受壓迫的　　people〔'pipḷ〕*n.* 國民；民族
> within〔wɪð'ɪn〕*prep.* 在…之內
> earshot〔'ɪrˏʃɑt〕*n.* 聽力所及的範圍　　leader〔'lidɚ〕*n.* 領袖
> appeal〔ə'pil〕*v.* 要求；懇求　　*appeal to* 要求；呼籲
> treasure〔'trɛʒɚ〕*v.* 珍惜　　right〔raɪt〕*n.* 權利
> *human rights* 人權　　form〔fɔrm〕*n.* 形式
> oppression〔ə'prɛʃən〕*n.* 壓迫

2. (**E**) 依句意，選 (E) *admirable*〔'ædmərəbḷ〕*adj.* 可欽佩的；值得稱讚的。

3. (**C**) 他要求他們珍惜自己的人權，並「反抗」任何形式的壓迫，選 (C) *rise up against*「反抗」。　　rise〔raɪz〕*v.* 反抗；起義

He did this in Chile, Cuba and the Philippines, as well as in his
[4](I) homeland, Poland.
他曾在智利、古巴和菲律賓，以及他的家鄉波蘭這樣做。

> Chile〔'tʃɪlɪ〕*n.* 智利　　Cuba〔'kjubə〕*n.* 古巴
> Philippines〔'fɪləˏpinz〕*n. pl.* 菲律賓群島
> *as well as* 以及

4. (**I**) *homeland*〔'homˏlænd〕*n.* 家鄉

This was also a Pope who could spring surprises. As a Pope from a town full of Jews, he felt a special [5](H) obligation to respect them and was the first Pope to push a folded prayer-note between the stones of the Wailing Wall in Jerusalem.

這位教宗還會突然宣佈令人驚訝的事。身為教宗的他,是來自住滿猶太人的小鎮,所以他覺得特別有義務要尊重猶太人,而他也是第一位將摺起來的祈禱文,放入耶路撒冷的哭牆石縫中的教宗。

spring〔sprɪŋ〕v. 突然宣佈
surprise〔sə'praɪz〕n. 令人驚訝的事
Jew〔dʒu〕n. 猶太人　　respect〔rɪ'spɛkt〕v. 尊重
push〔puʃ〕v. 推進;擠　　folded〔'foldɪd〕adj. 摺疊的
prayer〔prɛr〕n. 祈禱文
note〔not〕n. 短箋;紙條　　stone〔ston〕n. 石頭
Wailing Wall 哭牆【耶路撒冷城內的一道牆,猶太人群集在此祈禱和哀悼】
Jerusalem〔dʒə'rusələm〕n. 耶路撒冷

5. (**H**) ***obligation***〔ˌɑblə'geʃən〕n. 義務

In 2000, [6](F) startlingly, he read out a long apology for the church's bad behavior over the centuries. Some noted that it was church members, [7](J) not the church itself, for whom he apologized.

令人驚訝的是,他在二○○○年時,為了教會幾世紀來的惡行,朗讀了一長串道歉的話。有些人發覺,他是為了教會成員而道歉,不是為了教會本身。

read out 朗誦;宣讀　　apology〔ə'pɑlədʒɪ〕n. 道歉
behavior〔bɪ'hevjɚ〕n. 行為

century ('sɛntʃərɪ) *n.* 世紀　　note (not) *v.* 發覺；注意到
member ('mɛmbɚ) *n.* 成員
apologize (ə'pɑləˌdʒaɪz) *v.* 道歉

6. (**F**) *startlingly* ('stɑrtḷɪŋlɪ) *adv.* 令人驚訝的是

7. (**J**) A, *not* B 是 A，不是 B (= *not B but A*)

[8](G) Nonetheless, it was a rare marvel that a man so certain of the church's possession of the truth should criticize those who had believed it with equal enthusiasm.

儘管如此，一個非常確信教會擁有真理的人，竟然會批評那些同樣熱中相信這件事的人，真是不可思議。

rare (rɛr) *adj.* 極度的；超乎尋常的；罕見的
marvel ('mɑrvḷ) *n.* 令人驚奇的事；不可思議的事
certain ('sɝtṇ) *adj.* 確信的　　possession (pə'zɛʃən) *n.* 擁有
truth (truθ) *n.* 真理　　should (ʃud) *aux.* 竟然
criticize ('krɪtəˌsaɪz) *v.* 批評
equal ('ikwəl) *adj.* 同樣的；相等的
enthusiasm (ɪn'θjuzɪˌæzəm) *n.* 熱中；狂熱

8. (**G**) *nonetheless* (ˌnʌnðə'lɛs) *adv.* 儘管如此

The greatest surprise, however, was the strength of spirit that kept him going. He carried on largely in order to [9](A) display, to a cynical world, the power of God at work in him and the needlessness of the fear of death.

　　但是，最令人驚訝的，是讓他不斷前進的精神力量。他會繼續做下去，大多是爲了向這個悲觀的世界，展示上帝對他的影響力，並告訴世人不必怕死。

> strength〔strɛŋθ〕*n.* 力量
>
> spirit〔'spɪrɪt〕*n.* 精神　　　***carry on*** 繼續（做）
>
> largely〔'lɑrdʒlɪ〕*adv.* 主要地；大多
>
> ***in order to*** 爲了　　　largely〔'lɑrdʒlɪ〕*adv.* 主要地；大多
>
> cynical〔'sɪnɪkl̩〕*adj.* 悲觀的；憤世嫉俗的
>
> power〔'pauɚ〕*n.* 力量　　　***at work*** 產生影響
>
> needlessness〔'nidlɪsnɪs〕*n.* 不必；不需要
>
> fear〔fɪr〕*n.* 害怕　　　death〔dɛθ〕*n.* 死亡

9. (**A**) 依句意，大多是爲了向這個悲觀的世界「展示」上帝對他的影響力，選 (A) ***display***〔dɪ'sple〕*v.* 展示。

[10](**B**) Now that he has passed away, his bruised and worried church feels, more than anything, the lack of his confidence.

由於他已經過世，他的教會既傷心又擔憂，而且覺得最缺乏的，就是他的信心。

> ***pass away*** 逝世（ = *die* ）　　　bruised〔bruzd〕*adj.* 傷心的
>
> worried〔'wɜɪd〕*adj.* 擔心的
>
> ***more than anything*** 甚於其他任何事物；最…
>
> lack〔læk〕*n.* 缺乏　　　confidence〔'kɑnfədəns〕*n.* 信心

10. (**B**) 依句意，「由於」他已經過世，他的教會既傷心又擔憂，選
(B) ***now that***「由於；既然」。

TEST 36

說明：第 1 至 10 題，每題一個空格。請依文意在文章後所提供的 (A) 到 (J) 選項中分別選出最適當者。

For people who like to keep poultry, ducks offer certain advantages ___1___ hens. Ducks are ___2___ to some common diseases found in hens and are less vulnerable to others. Some breeds of duck produce bigger eggs than hens. In addition, ducks lay eggs over a longer season than ___3___ hens.

Poultry keepers ___4___ gardens have less to worry about if they keep ducks rather than hens because ___5___ are less apt to dig up plants and roots. While both hens and ducks benefit the garden by eating pests, hens are known to damage herb and grass beds. Ducks, ___6___, will search for insects and snails more carefully.

When keeping ducks, one has to consider just how many the land will ___7___. Generally the rule is 100 ducks per half hectare. If more than this ___8___ is introduced, there is a risk of compacting the soil, ___9___ can lead to muddy conditions for long periods as the rain is not easily ___10___ into the ground. 【北模】

(A) absorbed   (B) support   (C) which
(D) do   (E) over   (F) on the other hand
(G) proportion   (H) with   (I) the former
(J) immune

TEST 36 詳解

For people who like to keep poultry, ducks offer certain
advantages [1](E) over hens. Ducks are [2](J) immune to some common
diseases found in hens and are less vulnerable to others.

對於喜歡養家畜的人來說，鴨子在某些地方是優於母雞的。鴨子對於
某些在母雞身上常見的疾病有免疫力，而且也比較不容易感染其他疾病。

keep〔kip〕v. 飼養　　poultry〔'poltrɪ〕n. 家禽
duck〔dʌk〕n. 鴨子　　offer〔'ɔfɚ〕v. 有；提供
certain〔'sɝtn̩〕adj. 某些
advantage〔əd'væntɪdʒ〕n. 優點；優勢
hen〔hɛn〕n. 母雞
common〔'kɑmən〕adj. 常見的
disease〔dɪ'ziz〕n. 疾病
vulnerable〔'vʌlnərəbl̩〕adj. 易受傷的；易感染的

1. (**E**) 依句意，鴨子在某些地方是「優於」母雞的，選 (E) ***over***
〔'ovɚ〕prep. 高於；超過。
have an advantage over 勝過；比某人佔優勢

2. (**J**) 依句意，鴨子對於某些在母雞身上常見的疾病「有免疫力」，
選 (J) ***immune***〔ɪ'mjun〕adj. 有免疫力的。

Some breeds of duck produce bigger eggs than hens. In addition,
ducks lay eggs over a longer season than [3](D) do hens.

有些品種的鴨子，生出來的蛋比雞蛋還大。此外，鴨子下蛋的時期比母
雞來得長。

breed〔brid〕*n.* 品種　　produce〔prə'djus〕*v.* 生產

in addition 此外

lay〔le〕*v.* 下（蛋）（三態變化為：lay-laid-laid）

over〔'ovə〕*prep.* 在…期間　　season〔'sizn〕*n.* 時期；季節

3. (**D**) 代替動詞 lay，可用助動詞 ***do***，故選 (D)。

Poultry keepers **⁴(H) with** gardens have less to worry about if they keep ducks rather than hens because **⁵(I) the former** are less apt to dig up plants and roots.

　有庭園的家禽飼主，如果養鴨而不養雞的話，也比較不用擔心，因為前者比較不會把植物和根挖出來。

keeper〔'kipə〕*n.* 飼主

garden〔'gɑrdn〕*n.* 庭園；花園；果園；菜圃

worry〔'wɝɪ〕*v.* 擔心　　***rather than*** 而不是

apt〔æpt〕*adj.* 可能會…的　　***be apt to V.*** 易於；傾向於

dig〔dɪg〕*v.* 挖　　***dig up*** 挖出

plant〔plænt〕*n.* 植物　　root〔rut〕*n.* 根

4. (**H**) 依句意，「有」庭園，選 (H) ***with***。

5. (**I**) 因為「前者」比較不會把植物和根挖出來，選 (I) ***the former*** 「前者」。

While both hens and ducks benefit the garden by eating pests, hens are known to damage herb and grass beds. Ducks, **⁶(F) on the other hand**, will search for insects and snails more carefully.

儘管母雞和鴨子都吃害蟲，所以都對庭園有利，但是母雞卻以破壞草本植物和青草的苗圃爲人所知。另一方面，鴨子則會比較小心地搜尋昆蟲和蝸牛。

benefit (＇bɛnəfɪt) *v.* 有益於　　pest (pɛst) *n.* 害蟲

known (non) *adj.* 爲…所知的

damage (＇dæmɪdʒ) *v.* 損害；破壞

herb (hɝb , ɝb) *n.* 藥草；草本植物　　grass (græs) *n.* 草

bed (bɛd) *n.* 苗圃；花圃　　***search for*** 尋找

insect (＇ɪnsɛkt) *n.* 昆蟲　　snail (snel) *n.* 蝸牛

6. (**F**) 依句意，「另一方面」，鴨子則會比較小心地搜尋昆蟲和蝸牛，
選 (F) ***on the other hand*** 「另一方面」。

When keeping ducks, one has to consider just how many the
land will [7]**(B) support**. Generally the rule is 100 ducks per half
hectare.

養鴨的時候，你只需要考慮這塊地可以養得起多少隻鴨子。通常慣例是每半公頃可以養一百隻鴨子。

consider (kən＇sɪdɚ) *v.* 考慮

generally (＇dʒɛnərəlɪ) *adv.* 通常

rule (rul) *n.* 慣例　　per (pɝ) *prep.* 每…

half (hæf) *adj.* 一半的　　hectare (＇hɛktɛr) *n.* 公頃

7. (**B**) 依句意，你只需要考慮這塊地可以「養得起」多少隻鴨子，
選 (B) ***support*** (sə＇port) *v.* 扶養；供養。

If more than this [8](G) *proportion is introduced*, there is a risk of compacting the soil, [9](C) *which* can lead to muddy conditions for long periods *as the rain is not easily* [10](A) *absorbed into the ground*.

如果引進的比例超過這個數目，土壤就有被壓得十分結實的風險，這樣會導致這塊地長期處於泥濘的狀態，因為雨水不容易被土地吸收。

*　註：本句是個長句，文法分析如下：

　　　If 引導的副詞子句，表條件，修飾主要動詞 is。關係代名詞
　　　which 引導非限定形容詞子句，修飾前面所說過的整句話。
　　　as 引導副詞子句，表示原因，修飾 lead。

　　introduce〔͵ɪntrə'djus〕*v.* 引進；帶來
　　risk〔rɪsk〕*n.* 風險
　　compact〔kəm'pækt〕*v.* 使…結實；使…緊密
　　soil〔sɔɪl〕*n.* 土壤　　*lead to* 導致
　　muddy〔'mʌdɪ〕*adj.* 泥濘的
　　condition〔kən'dɪʃən〕*n.* 狀況；狀態
　　period〔'pɪrɪəd〕*n.* 期間；時期
　　ground〔graʊnd〕*n.* 地面；土地

8. (**G**) 如果引進的「比例」超過這個數目，選 (G) *proportion*
　　〔prə'porʃən〕*n.* 比例。

9. (**C**) 本句缺少一個連接詞，前有逗號，只有 *which* 可引導非限定
　　用法的形容詞子句，故選 (C)。

10. (**A**) 因為雨水不容易被土地「吸收」，選 (A) *absorbed*。
　　absorb〔əb'sɔrb〕*v.* 吸收

TEST 37

說明：第 1 至 10 題，每題一個空格。請依文意在文章後所提供的 (A) 到
(J) 選項中分別選出最適當者。

    The full-grown blue whale gets food   __1__   a
strange way. Some whales have teeth, but not the blue
whale. Instead, it has a kind of curtain that hangs from
the roof of its mouth. It *is* made of fine whalebone.
When the whale wants to feed, it opens its mouth   __2__
and swims full speed ahead. Soon its huge mouth is
  __3__   with water. In the water are thousands of tiny
sea animals and plants. The whale then closes its mouth
and pushes the water   __4__   with its tongue. The water
shoots out through the curtain. But the food stays in the
whale's mouth. It takes many mouthfuls to fill   __5__
such a big animal.

    For much of the year whales live in warm seas.
That is   __6__   baby whales are born. But warm waters
are not as rich in food as cold waters. So,   __7__   the
baby whales are strong enough, the whales move south.

Blue whales may swim ___8___ around the world to
reach the waters near the South Pole. Their ___9___ skin
helps them swim quickly. They rest ___10___ taking little
naps as they float on top of the water. Finally they reach
the cold sea, and the summer feast begins. 【台中一中複習考】

(A) when   (B) in   (C) wide   (D) up

(E) filled   (F) by   (G) where   (H) out

(I) smooth   (J) halfway

【劉毅老師的話】

　　平常練習做題目時，要養成計時的
習慣，訓練自己的速度，這樣考試時才
不會緊張。

TEST 37 詳解

The full-grown blue whale gets food **[1](B) in** a strange way. Some whales have teeth, but not the blue whale. Instead, it has a kind of curtain that hangs from the roof of its mouth.

發育完全的藍鯨以奇怪的方式覓食。有些鯨魚有牙齒，但是藍鯨沒有。取而代之的，是一種從上顎垂下來的簾狀構造。

> **full-grown** (ˈfulˈgron) *adj.* 發育完全的；成熟的
> **whale** (hwel) *n.* 鯨魚   **teeth** (tiθ) *n. pl.* 牙齒 (單數為 tooth (tuθ))
> **instead** (ɪnˈstɛd) *adv.* 作為替代
> **urtain** (ˈkɜtn) *n.* 簾狀物；幕狀物   **hang** (hæŋ) *v.* 垂；掛
> **roof** (ruf) *n.* 上顎   **mouth** (mauθ) *n.* 嘴巴

1. (**B**) 表「以～方式」，介系詞要用 *in*。

It is made of fine whalebone. When the whale wants to feed, it opens its mouth **[2](C) wide** and swims full speed ahead. Soon its huge mouth is **[3](E) filled** with water. In the water are thousands of tiny sea animals and plants.

它是由細長的鯨鬚所構成的。當鯨魚要吃東西時，牠會把嘴巴張大，然後全速前進。牠的大嘴很快就會裝滿水。水裡有數千個微小的海洋動植物。

> **be made of** 由…組成   **fine** (faɪn) *adj.* 細的；細長的
> **whalebone** (ˈhwelˌbon) *n.* 鯨鬚；鯨骨
> **feed** (fid) *v.* (動物) 吃東西   **speed** (spid) *n.* 速度
> **ahead** (əˈhɛd) *adv.* 向前   ***swim full speed ahead*** 全速向前游
> **huge** (hjudʒ) *adj.* 巨大的   ***thousands of*** 數以千計的
> **tiny** (ˈtaɪnɪ) *adj.* 微小的   **plant** (plænt) *n.* 植物

2. (**C**) 牠會把嘴巴「張大」，選 (C) *wide*〔waɪd〕*adv.* 張大地。

3. (**E**) 依句意，牠的大嘴很快就會「裝滿」水，選 (E) *filled*。

The whale then closes its mouth and pushes the water ⁴(H) out with its tongue. The water shoots out through the curtain. But the food stays in the whale's mouth. It takes many mouthfuls to fill ⁵(D) up such a big animal.

然後鯨魚會把嘴巴閉上，然後用舌頭把水推出來。水會通過簾狀構造射出來。但是食物卻留在鯨魚的嘴裡。要餵飽這麼大型的動物，需要吃很多口食物。

> push〔puʃ〕*v.* 推　　tongue〔tʌŋ〕*n.* 舌頭
> shoot〔ʃut〕*v.* 射出　　through〔θru〕*prep.* 通過；穿過
> take〔tek〕*v.* 需要　　mouthful〔'maʊθ,fʊl〕*n.* 一口的量
> fill〔fɪl〕*v.* 裝滿；填飽

4. (**H**) 然後鯨魚會把嘴巴閉上，然後用舌頭把水推「出來」，選 (H) *out*。

5. (**D**) 依句意，要餵「飽」這麼大型的動物，需要吃很多口食物，
　　　選 (D) *up*。　　*fill up* 裝滿；填飽

For much of the year whales live in warm seas. That is ⁶(G) where baby whales are born. But warm waters are not as rich in food as cold waters. So, ⁷(A) when the baby whales are strong enough, the whales move south.

鯨魚一年中有很多時間，都住在溫暖的海裡。鯨魚寶寶也是在那裡誕生的。但是溫暖海域中的食物，不像寒冷海域那麼豐富。所以當鯨魚寶寶夠強壯時，牠們就會向南遷移。

much〔 mʌtʃ 〕*pron.* 大量；許多
waters〔'wɑtəz 〕*n. pl.* 海域；水域　　rich〔 rɪtʃ 〕*adj.* 豐富的
be rich in 有豐富的⋯　　move〔 muv 〕*v.* 移動；遷移
south〔 saʊθ 〕*adv.* 向南方

6. (**G**) 表「地點」，關係副詞須用 ***where***。

7. (**A**)「當」鯨魚寶寶夠強壯時，牠們就會向南遷移，選 (A) ***when***。

Blue whales may swim ^{8}(**J**) halfway around the world to reach the
waters near the South Pole.　Their ^{9}(**I**) smooth skin helps them swim
quickly.　They rest ^{10}(**F**) by taking little naps as they float on top of the
water.　Finally they reach the cold sea, and the summer feast begins.

藍鯨可能要游遍半個地球，才能到達南極附近的海域。牠們身上的光滑皮
膚，有助於快速游動。當牠們浮在水面上時，會藉由小睡片刻來休息一下。
最後當牠們來到寒冷的海域時，夏季的盛宴就開始了。

reach〔 ritʃ 〕*v.* 到達　　　pole〔 pol 〕*n.* 極；極地
the South Pole 南極　　skin〔 skɪn 〕*n.* 皮膚
rest〔 rɛst 〕*v.* 休息　　　nap〔 næp 〕*n.* 小睡
take a nap 小睡片刻　　float〔 flot 〕*v.* 漂浮
on top of 在⋯的上面　　finally〔'faɪnḷɪ 〕*adv.* 最後
feast〔 fist 〕*n.* 盛宴

8. (**J**) 藍鯨可能要游遍「半個」地球，才能到達南極附近的海域，
　　　 選 (J) ***halfway***〔'hæf'we 〕*adv.* 到中途；到一半。

9. (**I**) ***smooth***〔 smuð 〕*adj.* 光滑的

10. (**F**) 依句意，當牠們浮在水面上時，會「藉由」小睡片刻來休息一下，
　　　 選 (F) ***by***。

TEST 38

說明：第 1 至 10 題，每題一個空格。請依文意在文章後所提供的 (A) 到
(J) 選項中分別選出最適當者。

"In Georgia, you must close your windows at night to
keep it out of the house," said James Dickey in his poem
Kudzu.

Kudzu is native to Japan and China; ___1___, it grows
much better in the Southeastern United States. The warm
climate there is so perfect for Kudzu ___2___ it can grow as
much as a ___3___ a day. Kudzu is a vine that when left
uncontrolled will eventually grow ___4___ almost any fixed
object, including other vegetation. Over a ___5___ of several
years, it will kill trees by ___6___ the sunlight. For this and
other reasons, people would like to get rid of it.

In the south, ___7___ the winters are moderate, the first
frost ___8___ kudzu into dead leaves, but the kudzu vine will
continue growing the next summer from where
it was ___9___ by cold weather the previous year. These vines
will cover buildings and parked vehicles in a few years if no
___10___ is made to control their growth. Many abandoned
houses, vehicles and barns covered with kudzu can be seen
in Georgia and other southern states. 【北模】

(A) over (B) that   (C) turns   (D) period   (E) effort
(F) foot (G) where (H) stopped (I) blocking (J) however

TEST 38 詳解

"In Georgia, you must close your windows at night to keep it out of the house," said James Dickey in his poem Kudzu.

「在喬治亞州,你晚上睡覺一定要關窗,才能把它阻擋在屋外,」詹姆斯・迪奇在他寫的「葛」這首詩中說。

> Georgia (ˈdʒɔrdʒə) *n.* 喬治亞州
> ***keep…out of*** 不讓…入內;阻擋…
> poem (ˈpo·ɪm) *n.* 詩　　kudzu (ˈkʊdzu) *n.* 葛

Kudzu is native to Japan and China; [1](J) however, it grows much better in the Southeastern United States. The warm climate there is so perfect for Kudzu [2](B) that it can grow as much as a [3](F) foot a day.

葛原產於日本和中國;但在美國東南部卻長得好多了。那裡溫暖的氣候非常適合葛,所以它一天可以長到一呎。

> native (ˈnetɪv) *adj.* 原產的　　***be native to*** 原產於
> southeastern (ˌsaʊθˈistən) *adj.* 東南的
> climate (ˈklaɪmɪt) *n.* 氣候
> perfect (ˈpɝfɪkt) *adj.* 完美的;最適合的　　grow (gro) *v.* 成長

1. (**J**) 依句意,選 (J) ***however***「然而」。

2. (**B**) ***so…that~***　如此…以致於~

3. (**F**) 依句意,它一天可以長到一「呎」,選 (F) ***foot*** (fʊt) *n.* 呎。

Kudzu is a vine that when left uncontrolled will eventually grow
[4](A) over almost any fixed object, including other vegetation. Over
a [5](D) period of several years, it will kill trees by [6](I) blocking the
sunlight. For this and other reasons, people would like to get rid
of it.

葛是一種藤蔓，如果不加以控制的話，最後幾乎在各種固定的物體上，包
括其他植物上面，都會長滿葛。經過幾年的時間，它就會因爲擋住陽光，
而殺死那些樹木。由於種種原因，所以人們想要消滅葛。

> vine〔vaɪn〕*n.* 藤蔓　　leave〔liv〕*v.* 使…處於某種狀態
> uncontrolled〔ˌʌnkənˈtrold〕*adj.* 不加控制的
> eventually〔ɪˈvɛntʃʊəlɪ〕*adv.* 最後　　fixed〔fɪkst〕*adj.* 固定的
> object〔ˈɑbdʒɪkt〕*n.* 物體　　including〔ɪnˈkludɪŋ〕*prep.* 包括
> vegetation〔ˌvɛdʒəˈteʃən〕*n.* 植物
> over〔ˈovɚ〕*prep.*（時間上）經過　　several〔ˈsɛvərəl〕*adj.* 幾個的
> sunlight〔ˈsʌnˌlaɪt〕*n.* 陽光　　reason〔ˈrizṇ〕*n.* 理由；原因
> ***get rid of*** 擺脫；消滅

4. (**A**) ***grow over*** 長滿

5. (**D**) 經過幾年的「時間」，選 (D) ***period***〔ˈpɪrɪəd〕*n.* 期間。

6. (**I**) 它就會因爲「擋住」陽光，而殺死那些樹木，選 (I)
　　　blocking。　　block〔blɑk〕*v.* 阻擋

In the south, [7](G) where the winters are moderate, the first frost
[8](C) turns kudzu into dead leaves, but the kudzu vine will continue
growing the next summer from where it was [9](H) stopped by cold
weather the previous year.

南部的冬天很溫和，第一次結的霜會把葛變成枯葉，但是到了隔年的夏天，葛的藤蔓又會從前一年因寒冷天氣而停止生長的地方，開始繼續長。

south〔 sauθ 〕*n.* 南方　　moderate〔'mɑdərɪt 〕*adj.* 溫和的
frost〔 frɔst 〕*n.* 霜　　dead〔 dɛd 〕*adj.* 枯萎的
leaves〔 livz 〕*n. pl.* 葉子（單數為 leaf〔 lif 〕）
continue〔 kən'tɪnju 〕*v.* 繼續　　weather〔'wɛðɚ 〕*n.* 天氣
previous〔'priviəs 〕*adj.* 之前的

7.（ **G** ）表「地點」，關係副詞須用 *where*。

8.（ **C** ）第一次結的霜會把葛「變成」枯葉，選 (C) *turns*。
　　　 turn A *into* B 把 A 變成 B

9.（ **H** ）葛的藤蔓又會從前一年因寒冷天氣而「停止」生長的地方，開始繼續生長，選 (H) *stopped*。

These vines will cover buildings and parked vehicles in a few years if no ^{10}(E) effort is made to control their growth. Many abandoned houses, vehicles and barns covered with kudzu can be seen in Georgia and other southern states.

如果不努力抑制它們生長，那麼在幾年之內，這些藤蔓就會覆蓋在建築物和停放的車輛上。在喬治亞州和南方其他各州，都可以看到很多被葛覆蓋的廢棄屋、車輛，和穀倉。

cover〔'kʌvɚ 〕*v.* 覆蓋　　parked〔 pɑrkt 〕*adj.* 停放的
vehicle〔'viɪkl̩ 〕*n.* 車輛　　control〔 kən'trol 〕*v.* 控制
growth〔 groθ 〕*n.* 生長　　abandoned〔 ə'bændənd 〕*adj.* 被拋棄的
barn〔 bɑrn 〕*n.* 穀倉；倉庫　　southern〔'sʌðɚn 〕*adj.* 南方的
state〔 stet 〕*n.* 州

10.（ **E** ）依句意，如果不「努力」抑制它們生長，選 (E) *effort*〔'ɛfɚt 〕*n.* 努力。

TEST 39

說明： 第 1 至 10 題，每題一個空格。請依文意在文章後所提供的 (A) 到 (J) 選項中分別選出最適當者。

Over the years many people have reported seeing mysterious objects in the sky. Sometimes these objects are ___1___ as having unusual bright lights. Some people even insist that they have been taken on board ___2___. They say they have also been given examinations and tests ___3___ their will. After they were returned home, many ___4___ anxiety and occasional flashbacks.

Yesterday evening, my friend Tom told me he had seen a flying saucer with a beam of light, and that he had seen an alien (creature) with a big head and small eyes, too. Frightened, he ___5___. When he woke up, he found himself lying on the road. Although his words gave me the ___6___, I could not believe him. But he ___7___ that he had undergone hypnosis to try to remember what really had happened. Still I thought it was not actual ___8___, for it is possible to remember "a dream." He's a boy with such a colorful ___9___ and he often makes up strange stories to ___10___ me. 【嘉義高中複習考】

(A) claimed (B) imagination (C) described (D) against
(E) creeps   (F) proof   (G) passed out (H) experienced
(I) play tricks on   (J) spaceships

TEST 39 詳解

Over the years many people have reported seeing mysterious objects in the sky. Sometimes these objects are [1](C) described as having unusual bright lights. Some people even insist that they have been taken on board [2](J) spaceships.

多年來，很多人都說，他們看過空中有神祕的物體。根據他們的描述，有時這些物體會有不尋常的亮光。有些人甚至堅稱，自己被帶上了太空船。

> ***over the years*** 多年來　　report〔rɪˋport〕v. 說；敘述
> mysterious〔mɪsˋtɪrɪəs〕*adj.* 神祕的
> object〔ˋɑbdʒɪkt〕*n.* 物體
> unusual〔ʌnˋjuʒʊəl〕*adj.* 不尋常的
> bright〔braɪt〕*adj.* 光亮的　　light〔laɪt〕*n.* 光
> insist〔ɪnˋsɪst〕*v.* 堅持；堅稱　　***on board*** 上（車、船、飛機等）

1. (**C**) 依句意，根據他們的「描述」，有時這些物體會有不尋常的亮光，選 (C) ***described***。　　describe〔dɪˋskraɪb〕*v.* 描述

2. (**J**) 有些人甚至堅稱，自己被帶上了「太空船」，選 (J) ***spaceships***。　　spaceship〔ˋspesˏʃɪp〕*n.* 太空船

They say they have also been given examinations and tests [3](D) against their will. After they were returned home, many [4](H) experienced anxiety and occasional flashbacks.

他們說自己還被迫做一些檢查和測試。許多人在返家之後，都有焦慮不安，以及偶爾想起過去畫面的經驗。

examination〔ɪɡ͵zæmə'neʃən〕*n.* 檢查　　will〔wɪl〕*n.* 意願
anxiety〔æŋ'zaɪətɪ〕*n.* 焦慮；不安
occasional〔ə'keʒən!〕*adj.* 偶爾的
flashback〔'flæʃ͵bæk〕*n.* 倒敘（回憶往事而重現過去的場面）

3.（ **D** ）*against one's will* 違背本意；無可奈何地

4.（ **H** ）許多人在返家之後，都有焦慮不安，以及偶爾想起過去畫面的「經驗」，選 (H)。　experience〔ɪk'spɪrɪəns〕*v.* 體驗；經歷

Yesterday evening, my friend Tom told me he had seen a flying saucer with a beam of light, and that he had seen an alien (creature) with a big head and small eyes, too. Frightened, he [5](G) passed out.

　　昨天晚上，我的朋友湯姆跟我說，他看過發出一束光線的飛碟，而且還看過大頭小眼睛的外星人（生物）。而且他當時因為受到驚嚇，所以就昏倒了。

flying〔'flaɪɪŋ〕*adj.* 會飛的；飛行的
saucer〔'sɔsɚ〕*n.* 碟狀物　　*flying saucer* 飛碟
beam〔bim〕*n.*（光）束　　alien〔'elɪən〕*n.* 外星人
creature〔'kritʃɚ〕*n.* 生物　　frightened〔'fraɪtn̩d〕*adj.* 受到驚嚇的

5.（ **G** ）而且他當時因為受到驚嚇，所以就「昏倒」了，選 (G) *passed out*。
pass out 昏過去

When he woke up, he found himself lying on the road. Although his words gave me the [6](E) creeps, I could not believe him. But he [7](A) claimed that he had undergone hypnosis to try to remember what really had happened.

當他醒來時，他發現自己躺在路上。雖然他的話令我毛骨悚然，我還是不相信他。但他宣稱自己接受過催眠，試圖要想起到底發生了什麼事。

> **wake up** 醒來
>
> lie〔laɪ〕*v.* 躺；臥（三態變化為：lie-lay-lain；現在分詞為 lying）
>
> undergo〔͵ʌndə'go〕*v.* 接受；經歷；遭遇
>
> hypnosis〔hɪp'nosɪs〕*n.* 催眠　　happen〔'hæpən〕*v.* 發生

6. (**E**) 依句意，雖然他的話令我「毛骨悚然」，我還是不相信他，
　　　　 選 (E) *creeps*〔krips〕*n. pl.* 毛骨悚然的感覺。

7. (**A**) 他「宣稱」自己接受過催眠，選 (A) *claimed*。
　　　　 claim〔klem〕*v.* 宣稱

Still I thought it was not actual [8](**F**) proof, for it is possible to remember "a dream."　He's a boy with such a colorful [9](**B**) imagination and he often makes up strange stories to [10](**I**) play tricks on me.

可是我還是覺得那不算實證，因為他可能想起「一個夢」。他是個想像力很豐富的男孩，而且他常常編奇怪的故事來騙我。

> still〔stɪl〕*adv.* 儘管如此還
>
> actual〔'æktʃuəl〕*adj.* 真實的　　possible〔'pɑsəbḷ〕*adj.* 可能的
>
> colorful〔'kʌləfəl〕*adj.* 豐富的　　**make up** 編造；捏造

8. (**F**) 可是我還是覺得那不算實「證」，選 (F) *proof*〔pruf〕*n.* 證據。

9. (**B**) 他是個「想像力」很豐富的男孩，選 (B) *imagination*
　　　　〔ɪ͵mædʒə'neʃən〕*n.* 想像力。

10. (**I**) *trick*〔trɪk〕*n.* 詭計；欺騙
　　　　play a trick on sb. 跟某人開玩笑；欺騙某人

TEST 40

說明： 第 1 至 10 題，每題一個空格。請依文意在文章後所提供的 (A) 到
(J) 選項中分別選出最適當者。

In many ways, talking is an art and we must not underestimate the effect of words. Well-used words become masterpieces, which can create and nourish. __1__, words shaped without thoughtful consideration can hurt and destroy, causing unbearable pain and deep regret.

So before we speak, perhaps it would be wise to first give __2__ thought to what we wish to say. Will it hurt anyone? Will it start an unnecessary dispute? Will it reopen old wounds? __3__ a few jokes or frank remarks are OK, many of us can't tell __4__ the thin line between acceptable and unacceptable is. What might seem a __5__ joke to us may send someone else over the edge. __6__, things of no real importance are often best left __7__. Wise are those who heed this fine rule of life and who talk little and carefully, for while we are perfectly free to give __8__ to our thoughts, we must not forget the rights of others — the right not to be made a laughingstock, to be __9__, and to enjoy the music of our __10__. 【北模】

(A) conversation (B) unsaid (C) careful (D) voice
(E) In fact (F) harmless (G) Although (H) respected
(I) However (J) where

TEST 40 詳解

In many ways, talking is an art and we must not underestimate the effect of words. Well-used words become masterpieces, which can create and nourish. [1](I) However, words shaped without thoughtful consideration can hurt and destroy, causing unbearable pain and deep regret.

談話在很多方面，都是一種藝術，所以我們不能低估談話的影響。用得精闢的話語，會變成能創造和滋養的傑作。然而，沒有經過深思熟慮的話，可能會傷人、帶來破壞，會造成無法忍受的痛苦，和深深的悔恨。

way〔we〕*n.* 方面
underestimate〔͵ʌndɚˈɛstəˌmet〕*v.* 低估
effect〔ɪˈfɛkt〕*n.* 影響　　masterpiece〔ˈmæstɚˌpis〕*n.* 傑作
create〔krɪˈet〕*v.* 創造　　nourish〔ˈnɝɪʃ〕*v.* 滋養
shape〔ʃep〕*v.* 使成形　　thoughtful〔ˈθɔtfəl〕*adj.* 深思的
consideration〔kənˌsɪdəˈreʃən〕*n.* 考慮
hurt〔hɝt〕*v.* 傷害　　destroy〔dɪˈstrɔɪ〕*v.* 破壞
cause〔kɔz〕*v.* 造成
unbearable〔ʌnˈbɛrəbl̩〕*adj.* 無法忍受的
pain〔pen〕*n.* 痛苦
deep〔dip〕*adj.* 深的　　regret〔rɪˈgrɛt〕*n.* 後悔

1. (I)　此處語氣有轉折，故選 (I) *However*「然而」。

So before we speak, perhaps it would be wise to first give [2](C) careful thought to what we wish to say. Will it hurt anyone? Will it start an unnecessary dispute? Will it reopen old wounds?

所以在我們開口之前，或許比較明智的做法是，先仔細想想要說的話。
這些話會傷害任何人嗎？會開啟無謂的爭端嗎？會再次撕開舊傷口嗎？

perhaps〔pəˈhæps〕*adv.* 或許   wise〔waɪz〕*adj.* 明智的
first〔fɜst〕*adv.* 先   ***give thought to*** 思考
wish to 想要（= *want to*）   start〔stɑrt〕*v.* 開始
unnecessary〔ʌnˈnɛsəˌsɛrɪ〕*adj.* 不必要的
dispute〔dɪˈspjut〕*n.* 爭論
reopen〔riˈopən〕*v.* 重新開啟   wound〔wund〕*n.* 傷口

2. (**C**) 依句意，先「仔細」想想要說的話，選 (C) ***careful***「小心的；
仔細的」。

³**(G) Although** a few jokes or frank remarks are OK, many of us can't
tell ⁴**(J) where** the thin line between acceptable and unacceptable is.
雖然一些笑話或是坦白的意見，都還過得去，但許多人不知道可接受和
不可接受之間的細微分界線在哪裡。

frank〔fræŋk〕*adj.* 坦白的   remark〔rɪˈmɑrk〕*n.* 評論；話
tell〔tɛl〕*v.* 知道；看出   thin〔θɪn〕*adj.* 細緻的
line〔laɪn〕*n.* 分界；界限   acceptable〔əkˈsɛptəbl̩〕*adj.* 可接受的
unacceptable〔ˌʌnəkˈsɛptəbl̩〕*adj.* 不能接受的

3. (**G**) 依句意，選 (G) ***Although***「雖然」。

4. (**J**) 依句意，細微的分界線「在哪裡」，選 (J) ***where***。

What might seem a ⁵**(F) harmless** joke to us may send someone else
over the edge. ⁶**(E) In fact**, things of no real importance are often
best left ⁷**(B) unsaid**.
對我們而言似乎沒有惡意的笑話，卻可能使別人抓狂。事實上，無關緊
要的事，最好別說出來。

send sb. over the edge 使某人發狂   leave〔liv〕*v.* 使處於…狀態

5. **(F)** 對我們而言似乎「沒有惡意的」笑話，選 (F) *harmless*
〔'hɑrmlɪs〕*adj.* 無害的；無惡意的。

6. **(E)** 依句意，選 (E) *In fact*「事實上」。

7. **(B)** 無關緊要的事，最好「別說出來」，選 (B) *unsaid*〔ʌn'sɛd〕
adj. 不說出來的。

Wise are those who heed this fine rule of life and who talk little and
carefully, for while we are perfectly free to give [8](D) voice to our
thoughts, we must not forget the rights of others —— the right not to
be made a laughingstock, to be [9](H) respected, and to enjoy the music
of our [10](A) conversation.

最有智慧的人，是那些會注意到這項生活細則，而且說話說得既少又謹慎
的人，因為當我們非常自由地發表意見時，我們絕不能忘記，別人也有權
利——有不想被當成笑柄的權利、有被尊重的權利，以及享受美妙談話的
權利。

> heed〔hid〕*v.* 注意　　fine〔faɪn〕*adj.* 細微的
> little〔'lɪtḷ〕*adv.* 幾乎不；很少
> perfectly〔'pɜfɪktlɪ〕*adv.* 完全地　　thoughts〔θɔts〕*n. pl.* 意見
> right〔raɪt〕*n.* 權利　　laughingstock〔'læfɪŋ,stɑk〕*n.* 笑柄
> music〔'mjuzɪk〕*n.* 和諧悅耳的聲音

8. **(D)** 因為當我們非常自由地「發表」意見時，選 (D) *voice*。
give voice to 發表

9. **(H)** 有被「尊重」的權利，選 (H) *respected*。
respect〔rɪ'spɛkt〕*v.* 尊重

10. **(A)** 以及享受美妙「談話」的權利，選 (A) *conversation*
〔,kɑnvə'seʃən〕*n.* 談話。

TEST 41

說明： 第 1 至 10 題，每題一個空格。請依文意在文章後所提供的 (A) 到 (J) 選項中分別選出最適當者。

It's not just men who love to watch TV sports; ___1___ around the world are getting in on the act, too. A survey of adult ___2___ in 34 countries reveals that 93% of men watching TV ___3___ in to sports. Among women, the number isn't all ___4___ far behind at 83%.

But ___5___ men and women are watching is rather different. Men are attracted primarily to soccer, American football, car racing and boxing. Women are more ___6___ than men to watch figure skating, tennis, gymnastics, athletics, volleyball and swimming, although some women are also attracted to soccer and American football. But both sexes ___7___ the same passion for baseball, ___8___ hockey and golf. Overall, soccer, ___9___ highest in 24 of 34 countries, reigns ___10___ the world's favorite TV sport. 【北模】

(A) likely   (B) as   (C) viewers   (D) as well as
(E) ranking   (F) women (G) that   (H) what
(I) share   (J) tune

TEST 41 詳解

It's not just men who love to watch TV sports; [1](F) women
around the world are getting in on the act, too.

不是只有男人喜歡看電視上的體育節目；全世界的女性也逐漸加
入了這個活動。

> ***around the world*** 全世界的
> ***get in on the act*** 加入行動

1. (**F**) 依句意，選 (F) ***women***「女性」。

A survey of adult [2](C) viewers in 34 countries reveals that 93% of
men watching TV [3](J) tune in to sports. Among women, the
number isn't all [4](G) that far behind at 83%.

一項針對三十四個國家的成年觀眾所做的調查顯示，在看電視的男性當
中，有百分之九十三會收看體育節目。而女性也沒有落後那麼多，數字是
百分之八十三。

> survey〔'sɜve〕*n.* 調查　　adult〔ə'dʌlt〕*adj.* 成年的
> reveal〔rɪ'vil〕*v.* 顯示　　***far behind*** 遠遠落後

2. (**C**) 針對三十四個國家的成年「觀眾」所做的調查顯示，
選 (C) ***viewers***。　　viewer〔'vjuɚ〕*n.* 觀眾

3. (**J**) 依句意，在看電視的男性當中，有百分之九十三會「收看」體育
節目，選 (J) ***tune***。　　***tune in to*** 收看；收聽 (頻道、節目等)

4. (**G**) 而女性也沒有落後「那麼」多，選 (G) ***that***。
all that 那麼

But [5](H) what men and women are watching is rather different. Men are attracted primarily to soccer, American football, car racing and boxing.

但是，男人和女人看的體育節目大不相同。男人大多愛看足球、美式足球、賽車，和拳擊。

> rather ('ræðɚ) *adv.* 相當地　　attract (ə'trækt) *v.* 吸引
> ***be attracted to ~*** 受～吸引
> primarily ('praɪ,mɛrəlɪ) *adv.* 主要地
> soccer ('sɑkɚ) *n.* 足球
> ***American football*** 美式足球；橄欖球
> ***car racing*** 賽車　　boxing ('bɑksɪŋ) *n.* 拳擊

5. (**H**) 空格應填複合關代 *what*，相當於 the things that 或 the things which。

Women are more [6](A) likely than men to watch figure skating, tennis, gymnastics, athletics, volleyball and swimming, although some women are also attracted to soccer and American football.

女人則比男人更有可能看花式溜冰、網球、體操、田徑、排球和游泳，雖然有些女性也很喜歡看足球和美式足球。

> ***figure skating*** 花式溜冰　　tennis ('tɛnɪs) *n.* 網球
> gymnastics (dʒɪm'næstɪks) *n.* 體操
> athletics (æθ'lɛtɪks) *n.* 田徑運動
> volleyball ('vɑlɪ,bɔl) *n.* 排球

6. (**A**) 依句意，女人則比男人更「有可能」看花式溜冰，選 (A) *likely* ('laɪklɪ) *adj.* 可能的。

But both sexes [7](I) share the same passion for baseball, [8](D) as well as hockey and golf. Overall, soccer, [9](E) ranking highest in 24 of 34 countries, reigns [10](B) as the world's favorite TV sport.

但兩性對於棒球，以及曲棍球和高爾夫球，則同樣喜愛。就整體而言，在三十四個國家中，足球排第一的國家有二十四個，足球是全世界的人最喜歡收看的電視運動。

> sex〔sɛks〕 *n.* 性別　　same〔sem〕*adj.* 同樣的
>
> passion〔'pæʃən〕 *n.* 熱情；愛好
>
> baseball〔'bes,bɔl〕 *n.* 棒球
>
> hockey〔'hakɪ〕 *n.* 曲棍球　　golf〔gɔlf〕 *n.* 高爾夫球
>
> overall〔,ovə'ɔl〕 *adv.* 就整體而言 (= *generally* = *on the whole*)
>
> reign〔ren〕 *v.* 稱霸；盛行；佔優勢
>
> favorite〔'fevərɪt〕 *adj.* 最喜歡的

7. (I) *share*〔ʃɛr〕*v.* 分享；同樣有

8. (D) as well as 字面意思是「和…一樣好」，在這裡是對等連接詞，作「以及」解。
   例：He gave me money *as well as* advice.
   　　（他給我錢以及忠告。）

9. (E) 足球「排」第一的國家有二十四個，選 (E) *ranking*。
   rank〔ræŋk〕*v.* 排名

10. (B) 足球是全世界的人最喜歡收看的電視運動，選 (B) *as*「作為；身為」。

TEST 42

說明： 第 1 至 10 題，每題一個空格。請依文意在文章後所提供的 (A) 到 (J) 選項中分別選出最適當者。

How free are the media? Well —— it varies from country to country. In countries like America and Sweden, there are very few limits on ___1___ journalists can report. Other governments are slightly ___2___ liberal. In Britain, ___3___, there is an "Official Secrets Act." This means that it is ___4___ the law to report certain sensitive information about defense or intelligence matters.

And then there's a ___5___ group of countries which control their media very strictly. In cases like this, broadcasters and journalists who ___6___ the law are frequently sent to prison or sometimes ___7___ killed.

Lack of freedom is a serious journalistic issue, but it is not the only one in the censorship debate. On the other ___8___ of the coin, some people believe journalists have ___9___ freedom. The argument here is that newspapers often ___10___ people's private lives and print sensational stories which are untrue. Should this be allowed to happen? 【北模】

(A) break   (B) too much   (C) side   (D) what

(E) less   (F) invade   (G) against   (H) third

(I) for example   (J) even

TEST 42 詳解

How free are the media? Well —— it varies from country to country. In countries like America and Sweden, there are very few limits on [1](D) what journalists can report. Other governments are slightly [2](E) less liberal.

媒體有多自由？嗯——各國都不一樣。在像美國和瑞典這樣的國家，很少限制記者可以報導的東西。而其他政府就稍微比較不自由。

media (ˈmidɪə) *n. pl.* 媒體 (單數為 medium (ˈmidɪəm))
well (wɛl) *interj.* 嗯　　vary (ˈvɛrɪ) *v.* 不同
vary from A *to* A 每個 A 都不同　　Sweden (ˈswidn̩) *n.* 瑞典
limit (ˈlɪmɪt) *n.* 限制　　journalist (ˈdʒɜ·nl̩ɪst) *n.* 新聞記者
report (rɪˈport) *v.* 報導　　government (ˈgʌvə·nmənt) *n.* 政府
slightly (ˈslaɪtlɪ) *adv.* 稍微　　liberal (ˈlɪbərəl) *adj.* 自由的

1. (**D**) 依句意，很少限制記者可以報導的「東西」，選 (D) *what*。
2. (**E**) 而其他政府就稍微「比較不」自由，選 (E) *less*。

In Britain, [3](I) for example, there is an "Official Secrets Act." This means that it is [4](G) against the law to report certain sensitive information about defense or intelligence matters.

例如，英國有「官方秘密法」。意思是說，把有關國防的某些機密資訊，或情報機關的事情報導出來，是違法的。

Britain (ˈbrɪtən) *n.* 英國　　official (əˈfɪʃəl) *adj.* 官方的
secret (ˈsikrɪt) *n.* 秘密　　act (ækt) *n.* 法令；條例
mean (min) *v.* 意思是　　law (lɔ) *n.* 法律
certain (ˈsɜ·tn̩) *adj.* 某些　　sensitive (ˈsɛnsətɪv) *adj.* 有關國家機密的
defense (dɪˈfɛns) *n.* 國防
intelligence (ɪnˈtɛlədʒəns) *n.* 情報；情報機關
matter (ˈmætə·) *n.* 事情

3. (**I**) *for example* 例如

4. (**G**) 依句意，把有關國防的某些機密資訊，或情報機關的事情報導
出來，是「違」法的，選 (G) *against*〔əˈgɛnst〕*prep.* 違反。

And then there's a [5](**H**) third group of countries which control
their media very strictly. In cases like this, broadcasters and
journalists who [6](**A**) break the law are frequently sent to prison or
sometimes [7](**J**) even killed.

此外，還有第三類國家，他們會嚴格控管媒體。在像這樣的例子裡，
犯法的廣播者和記者，經常會被抓去坐牢，有時候甚至還會被殺害。

then〔ðɛn〕*adv.* 此外　　group〔grup〕*n.* 類；群
control〔kənˈtrol〕*v.* 控制　　strictly〔ˈstrɪktlɪ〕*adv.* 嚴格地
case〔kes〕*n.* 事例；實例
broadcaster〔ˈbrod,kæstə〕*n.* 電視台；廣播者
frequently〔ˈfrikwəntlɪ〕*adv.* 經常　　send〔sɛnd〕*v.* 送
prison〔ˈprɪzn̩〕*n.* 監獄　　kill〔kɪl〕*v.* 殺死

5. (**H**) 此外，還有「第三」類國家，他們會嚴格控管媒體，選 (H) *third*。

6. (**A**) 依句意，「犯」法的廣播者和記者，經常會被抓去坐牢，
選 (A) *break*〔brek〕*v.* 違反；觸犯。

7. (**J**) 有時候「甚至」還會被殺害，選 (J) *even*。

Lack of freedom is a serious journalistic issue, but it is not the
only one in the censorship debate. On the other [8](**C**) side of the
coin, some people believe journalists have [9](**B**) too much freedom.

缺乏自由是個重要的新聞議題，但它並非審查制度中的唯一爭論。
另一方面，有些人認為記者太自由了。

> lack〔læk〕*n.* 缺乏　　freedom〔'fridəm〕*n.* 自由
> serious〔'sɪrɪəs〕*adj.* 嚴重的；重要的
> journalistic〔ˌdʒɝnḷ'ɪstɪk〕*adj.* 新聞業的
> issue〔'ɪʃjʊ〕*n.* 議題
> censorship〔'sɛnsəʃɪp〕*n.* 審查（制度）
> debate〔dɪ'bet〕*n.* 爭論　　coin〔kɔɪn〕*n.* 硬幣

8. (**C**) *the other side of the coin*　（事情的）另一面；反面觀點

9. (**B**) 依句意，另一方面，有些人認為記者「太」自由了，
　　　　選 (B) *too much*。

The argument here is that newspapers often [10](F) invade people's
private lives and print sensational stories which are untrue.　Should
this be allowed to happen?

爭論點是在於，報紙常常侵擾人們的私生活，而且會刊登聳人聽聞的不實
報導。我們應該允許這種事發生嗎？

> argument〔'ɑrgjəmənt〕*n.* 爭論
> private〔'praɪvɪt〕*adj.* 私人的　　print〔prɪnt〕*v.* 刊登
> sensational〔sɛn'seʃənḷ〕*adj.* 誇張的；聳人聽聞的
> story〔'storɪ〕*n.* 新聞報導
> untrue〔ʌn'tru〕*adj.* 不真實的；假的　　allow〔ə'laʊ〕*v.* 允許

10. (**F**) 報紙常常「侵擾」人們的私生活，選 (F) *invade*〔ɪn'ved〕*v.*
　　　　侵害；侵擾。

TEST 43

說明： 第 1 至 10 題，每題一個空格。請依文意在文章後所提供的 (A) 到 (J) 選項中分別選出最適當者。

One of the saddest observations I have is this: many of us are ___1___ to learn from the people closest to us —— our parents, spouses, children, and friends. Rather than being ___2___ to learning, we close ourselves off out of fear, stubbornness or pride. It's almost as if we say to ___3___, "I have already learned all that I can learn. There is nothing ___4___ I need to learn."

It's sad, because often the people closest to us know us the best and can offer very simple ___5___. If we are too proud or stubborn to learn, we lose out on some wonderful, simple ways to ___6___ our lives.

I have tried to remain open to the suggestions of my friends and family. In fact, I have gone so ___7___ as to ask my family and friends, "What are some of my shortcomings?" Not only ___8___ this make the person you are asking feel wanted and special, but you end up getting some terrific advice. It's such a simple shortcut for growth, ___9___ few people use it. All it takes is a little ___10___ and humility, and the ability to let go of your ego. 【北模】

(A) does   (B) far   (C) else   (D) solutions
(E) courage   (F) reluctant   (G) ourselves   (H) yet
(I) improve   (J) open

TEST 43 詳解

One of the saddest observations I have is this: many of us are
[1](F) reluctant to learn from the people closest to us —— our parents,
spouses, children, and friends.

根據我的觀察，最悲哀的事情之一，就是：我們當中有許多人，不願
意向最親近的人學習 —— 也就是我們的父母、配偶、子女和朋友。

> observation〔ˌɑbzɚˈveʃən〕*n.* 觀察
> close〔klos〕*adj.* 親近的 < *to* >
> spouse〔spauz〕*n.* 配偶

1. (**F**) 依句意，「不願意」向最親近的人學習，選 (F) *reluctant*
〔rɪˈlʌktənt〕*adj.* 不願意的；不情願的 (= *unwilling*)。

Rather than being [2](J) open to learning, we close ourselves off out
of fear, stubbornness or pride. It's almost as if we say to
[3](G) ourselves, "I have already learned all that I can learn. There
is nothing [4](C) else I need to learn."

由於恐懼、固執或自尊，我們將自己封閉起來，而不願敞開心胸學習。
這簡直就像對自己說：「我已經學完所有能學的東西了。我不需要學其
它任何東西了。」

> *rather than* 而非   *close off* 封鎖；隔離
> *out of* 出於；由於   fear〔fɪr〕*n.* 恐懼
> stubbornness〔ˈstʌbɚnnɪs〕*n.* 固執   pride〔praɪd〕*n.* 自尊；驕傲

2. (**J**) *be open to learning* 敞開心胸學習

3. (**G**) 這簡直就像對「自己」說，須用反身代名詞 *ourselves*，選 (G)。

4. (**C**) 依句意，我不需要學「其他」任何東西了，選 (C) *else*。

It's sad, because often the people closest to us know us the best and can offer very simple ⁵(**D**) solutions. If we are too proud or stubborn to learn, we lose out on some wonderful, simple ways to ⁶(**I**) improve our lives.

這是很悲哀的，因為和我們最親近的人，常是最了解我們的人，他們能提供非常簡單的解決方法。如果我們太驕傲或太固執，而不願意學習，我們就無法獲得一些又好、又簡單的方法，來改善生活。

> offer〔'ɔfɚ〕*v.* 提供　　*too~to V.* 太~而不…
> proud〔praʊd〕*adj.* 驕傲的　　stubborn〔'stʌbɚn〕*adj.* 頑固的
> *lose out* 蒙受損失；未能獲得 <*on*>

5. (**D**) *solution*〔sə'luʃən〕*n.* 解決之道

6. (**I**) *improve*〔ɪm'pruv〕*v.* 改善

I have tried to remain open to the suggestions of my friends and family. In fact, I have gone so ⁷(**B**) far as to ask my family and friends, "What are some of my shortcomings?"

我對於朋友和家人的建議，一直努力保持開放的態度。事實上，我甚至會問我的家人和朋友，「我的缺點有哪些？」

> remain〔rɪ'men〕*v.* 保持　　suggestion〔sʌ'dʒɛstʃən〕*n.* 建議
> shortcoming〔'ʃɔrt͵kʌmɪŋ〕*n.* 缺點

7. (**B**) *go so far as to V.* 甚至～；竟然～

Not only [8](A) does this make the person you are asking feel wanted and special, but you end up getting some terrific advice. It's such a simple shortcut for growth, [9](H) yet few people use it. All it takes is a little [10](E) courage and humility, and the ability to let go of your ego.

這不只會讓被你詢問的對象，覺得被需要、覺得自己很特別，而且你最後也可以得到一些很棒的忠告。這是如此簡單的成長捷徑，但卻很少有人利用。你只需要一點點勇氣和謙虛，以及能夠放下自我的能力。

> ***end up*** 最後　　terrific〔tə'rɪfɪk〕*adj.* 很棒的
> advice〔əd'vaɪs〕*n.* 勸告　　shortcut〔'ʃɔrtˌkʌt〕*n.* 捷徑
> growth〔groθ〕*n.* 成長　　humility〔hju'mɪlətɪ〕*n.* 謙虛
> ability〔ə'bɪlətɪ〕*n.* 能力
> take〔tek〕*v.* 需要　　***let go of*** 放開
> ego〔'igo〕*n.* 自我；自尊

8. (**A**) not only…but also 是對等連接詞，also 可以省略，not only 放在句首，加強語氣時，一定要把 be 動詞或助動詞，放在主詞前倒裝。【詳見文法寶典 p.467】
　　　例：***Not only*** is he dependable, ***but*** (also) he is trustworthy.
　　　　　（他不僅可靠，而且值得信賴。）

9. (**H**) *yet*〔jɛt〕*conj.* 但是

10. (**E**) *courage*〔'kɝɪdʒ〕*n.* 勇氣

心得筆記欄

心得筆記欄

劉毅英文家教班成績優異同學獎學金排行榜

姓 名	學 校	總金額	姓 名	學 校	總金額	姓 名	學 校	總金額
潘羽薇	丹鳳高中	21100	高士權	建國中學	7600	賴奕均	松山高中	3900
孔為亮	中崙高中	20000	吳鴻鑫	中正高中	7333	戴寧昕	師大附中	3500
吳文心	北一女中	17666	謝宜廷	樹林高中	7000	江紫寧	大同高中	3500
賴柏盛	建國中學	17366	翁子惇	縣格致中學	6900	游清心	師大附中	3500
劉記齊	建國中學	16866	朱浩廷	陽明高中	6500	陳秦	海山高中	3500
張庭碩	建國中學	16766	張毓	成淵高中	6500	曾清翎	板橋高中	3400
陳瑾慧	北一女中	16700	吳宇珊	景美女中	6200	吳昕儒	中正高中	3400
羅培恩	建國中學	16666	王昱翔	延平高中	6200	高正岳	方濟高中	3250
毛威凱	建國中學	16666	張祐誠	林口高中	6100	林夏竹	新北高中	3100
王辰方	北一女中	16666	游需晴	靜修女中	6000	曾昭惠	永平高中	3000
李俊逸	建國中學	16666	林彥君	大同高中	6000	萬彰允	二信高中	3000
溫彥瑜	建國中學	16666	張騰升	松山高中	6000	張晨	麗山國中	3000
葉乃元	建國中學	16666	陳姿穎	縣格致中學	5900	廖泓恩	松山工農	3000
邱御碩	建國中學	16666	沈怡	復興高中	5800	張意涵	中正高中	2900
劉楫坤	松山高中	14400	莊永瑋	中壢高中	5600	劉冠伶	格致高中	2900
張凱俐	中山女中	13333	邱鈺璘	成功高中	5600	鄭翔文	格致高中	2800
邱馨荷	北一女中	12000	許斯閔	丹鳳高中	5500	莊益昕	建國中學	2700
陳瑾瑜	北一女中	11700	郭子豪	師大附中	5400	葉禹岑	成功高中	2700
施哲凱	松山高中	10450	黃韻蓉	東吳大學	5400	李承紘	復興高中	2600
陳宇翔	成功高中	10333	陸冠宏	師大附中	5200	林郁婷	北一女中	2600
林上軒	政大附中	10000	李柏霆	明倫高中	5100	張淨雅	北一女中	2600
陳玟好	中山女中	9000	孫廷瑋	成功高中	5100	許茵茵	東山高中	2600
林伽欣	格致高中	8800	李泓霖	松山高中	5000	范容菲	慧燈高中	2500
黃教頤	大同高中	8600	劉若白	大同高中	5000	孔為鳴	高 中 生	2500
蘇玉如	北一女中	8400	洪菀妤	師大附中	5000	廖永皓	大同高中	2500
廖奕翔	松山高中	8333	洪宇謙	成功高中	5000	蘇翊文	格致高中	2300
廖克軒	成功高中	8333	黃柏誠	師大附中	5000	陳歡	景文高中	2300
呂承翰	師大附中	8333	劉其瑄	中山女中	5000	邱國正	松山高中	2300
鮑其鈺	師大附中	8333	陳韋廷	成功高中	5000	許晉嘉	成功高中	2200
簡珞帆	高 中 生	8333	李維任	成功高中	5000	林靜宜	蘭陽女中	2200
蕭羽涵	松山高中	8333	林晉陽	師大附中	4900	吳玟慧	格致高中	2200
廖奕翔	松山高中	8333	林品君	北一女中	4900	吳珮彤	再興高中	2100
蕭若浩	師大附中	8333	柯季欣	華江高中	4500	張榕	南港高中	2000
連偉宏	師大附中	8333	李智傑	松山高中	4300	張媛瑄	景美女中	2000
王舒亭	縣格致中學	8300	許博勳	松山高中	4300	胡明媛	復興高中	2000
楊政勳	中和高中	8100	張鈞堯	新北高中	4166	盧世軒	縣鳳中學國中部	2000
鄭鈺立	建國中學	8000	林子薰	中山女中	4000	陳新雅	新北高中	2000
吳宇晏	南港高中	8000	王思予	林口高中	4000	黃子晏	私立大同高中	2000
楊沐焙	師大附中	7750	鄭宇彤	樹林高中	4000	蔡雅淳	秀峰高中	2000
謝育姍	景美女中	7600	張心瑜	格致高中	3900			

劉毅英文教育機構

台北本部：台北市許昌街17號6F（捷運M8出口對面・學善補習班）　　　TEL：（02）2389-5212
台中總部：台中市三民路三段125號7F（光南文具批發樓上・劉毅補習班）　　TEL：（04）2221-8861
www.learnschool.com.tw

指考文意選填

主　　　編 / 劉　毅

發　行　所 / 學習出版有限公司　　☎ (02) 2704-5525

郵 撥 帳 號 / 05127272 學習出版社帳戶

登　記　證 / 局版台業 *2179* 號

印　刷　所 / 裕強彩色印刷有限公司

台 北 門 市 / 台北市許昌街 10 號 2 F　　☎ (02) 2331-4060

台灣總經銷 / 紅螞蟻圖書有限公司　　☎ (02) 2795-3656

本公司網址　www.learnbook.com.tw

電 子 郵 件　learnbook@learnbook.com.tw

售價：新台幣二百二十元正

2016 年 8 月 1 日新修訂